"I love baking."

"Can't prove it by me," Max retorted. "We've worked together for over a week and I've seen two measly cookies. Kind of lame, Tina."

She laughed, and it felt good. They got to her door and she swung about, surprised. "That's the first time I've passed the café site without getting emotional. I didn't even realize we'd gone by."

"The company, perhaps?" Max bumped shoulders with her, a friendly gesture.

"Indubitably," she joked back, then looked up.

His eyes, his gaze…

Dark and questing, smiling and wondering.

He glanced down at her, then waited interminable seconds…for what? Her to move toward him?

She did.

His arms wrapped around her, tugging her close. The cool texture of his collar brushed her cheek, a contrast to the warmth he emanated.

He smelled like leather, dish soap and fresh lemons, a delightful mingling of scents in the chill of a Christmas-lit night.

Books by Ruth Logan Herne

Love Inspired

　Winter's End
　Waiting Out the Storm
　Made to Order Family
*Reunited Hearts
*Small-Town Hearts
*Mended Hearts
*Yuletide Hearts
*A Family to Cherish

*His Mistletoe Family
†The Lawman's Second Chance
†Falling for the Lawman
†The Lawman's Holiday Wish
†Loving the Lawman
　His Montana Sweetheart
†Her Holiday Family

*Men of Allegany County
†Kirkwood Lake

RUTH LOGAN HERNE

Born into poverty, Ruth puts great stock in one of her favorite Ben Franklinisms: "Having been poor is no shame. Being ashamed of it is." With God-given appreciation for the amazing opportunities abounding in our land, Ruth finds simple gifts in the everyday blessings of smudge-faced small children, bright flowers, freshly baked goods, good friends, family, puppies and higher education. She believes a good woman should never fear dirt, snakes or spiders, all of which like to infest her aged farmhouse, necessitating a good pair of tongs for extracting the snakes, a flat-bottomed shoe for the spiders, and for the dirt...

Simply put, she's learned that some things aren't worth fretting about! If you laugh in the face of dust and love to talk about God, men, romance, great shoes and wonderful food, feel free to contact Ruth through her website, www.ruthloganherne.com.

Her Holiday Family
Ruth Logan Herne

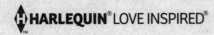
HARLEQUIN® LOVE INSPIRED®

Recycling programs
for this product may
not exist in your area.

ISBN-13: 978-0-373-87929-8

Her Holiday Family

For if you forgive others their trespasses,
your heavenly Father will also forgive you.
—*Matthew* 6:14

To the real Tina, one of the strongest and most amazing women I know. God blessed me the day we crossed paths in Denver, and He's continued to do so ever since. I love you, Teenster. And to Terry, Sean, Dan and Ronnie, my siblings who served when I was too young to understand the amazing sacrifice they made. Thank you. I love you. Your dedication is inspiration to so many!

Acknowledgments

Big thanks to Tony and Debby Giusti who are always willing to offer me advice on my military heroes. Your expertise is invaluable and I'm so grateful! To Melissa Endlich and Giselle Regus for their well-tuned advice about how to strengthen Tina and Max's story. Your advice produced a stronger book and I thank you! To Natasha Kern, my beloved agent, a woman with amazing patience and insight. I am so blessed to be working with you!

To Beth for all of her help and advice on how to write a better story. To the Seekers who are always there, ready to have my back as needed! To Basel's Restaurant, a fun, family style Greek restaurant here in upstate where I spent eleven years waiting tables. Real life is the VERY BEST research. And to Lakeshore Supply Company, our new local hardware store: I'm so glad you moved to town! Charlie Campbell's store came alive because of your delightful Hamlin and Hilton stores.

Chapter One

The old familiar voice stopped Tina Martinelli in her tracks as she stepped through the back door of Campbell's Hardware Store late Sunday morning. "I'll do whatever you need, Dad. I'm here to stay."

Max Campbell was here? In Kirkwood Lake?

Max Campbell, her teenage crush. The Campbell son who'd enlisted in the army and had never looked back. Max Campbell, the to-die-for, dark-haired, brown-eyed, adopted Latino son who'd broken countless hearts back in the day? The guy who used to hang out at her neighbor's house, until Pete Sawyer and his girlfriend lost their lives in a tragic late-night boating accident.

She'd never seen Max at the Sawyers' again. Not to visit Pete's parents. Not to offer Pete's little sister, Sherrie, a hug. Abnormally quiet became the new normal.

No more Max, no more Pete, no more parties.

A lot had changed on one warm, dark summer's night.

The wooden back door of Campbell's Hardware swung shut before she could stop it, the friendly squeak announcing her arrival. She did a very feminine mental reassessment before moving forward.

Hair?

Typical elfin crazy.

Nails?

Short and stubby, perfect for a hardware clerk, but not for coming face-to-face with Max Campbell over a decade later.

Makeup?

She hadn't bothered with any. She'd spent her early morning testing a new recipe, something she hoped to use in the not-too-distant future.

"Tina? That you?" The forced heartiness of Charlie Campbell's voice said she had little choice but to move forward, so that's what she did.

"I'm here, Charlie." She strode into the store, shoulders back, chin high, when what she wanted was a thirty-minute makeover. Why hadn't she worn her favorite jeans, the ones that made her feel young, jazzed and totally able to handle whatever life handed out?

Because you were coming to work in a hardware store, and who wears their best jeans to work in a hardware store?

The two men turned in tandem.

Her heart stopped when she locked eyes with Max.

She set it right back to beating with a stern internal warning because, despite Max's short, dark hair and dangerously attractive good looks, the guy had left his adoptive family when he'd finished college and hadn't come back since. And that was plain wrong.

"Tina, you remember our son Max, don't you?" Pride strengthened Charlie's voice, while the effects of his ongoing chemotherapy showed the reality of his current battle with pancreatic cancer. "He's a captain now, but he's come back home for a while."

"For good, Dad." Max's gaze offered assurance tinged with regret, but life taught Tina that assurances often meant little and ended badly. Around Kirkwood Lake the proof was in the pudding, as Jenny Campbell liked to say. And Max had a lot of proving to do.

She stepped forward and extended her hand, wishing her skin was smoother, her nails prettier, her—

He wrapped her hand in a broad, warm clasp, sure and strong but gentle, too.

And then he did the unthinkable.

He noticed her.

His gaze sharpened. His eyes widened. He gripped his other hand around the first, embracing her hand with both of his. "This is little Tina? Little Tina Martinelli? For real?"

The blush started somewhere around her toes and climbed quickly.

Little Tina.

That's what she'd been to him, an awestruck kid stargazing as the wretchedly good-looking youngest Campbell brother broke hearts across the lakeside villages. Max wasn't what you'd call a bad boy...

But no one accused him of being all that good, either.

"It's me." She flashed him a smile, hoping her Italian skin softened the blush, but the frankness of Charlie's grin said it hadn't come close. "I—"

"It's good to see you, Tina."

Warmth. Honesty. Integrity.

His tone and words professed all three, so maybe the army had done him good, but she'd locked down her teenage crush a long time back. Over. Done. Finished. "You, too."

Did he hold her hand a moment too long?

Of course not, he was just being nice.

But when she pulled her hand away, a tiny glint in his eye set her heart beating faster.

Clearly she needed a pacemaker, because she wasn't

about to let Max Campbell's inviting smile and good looks tempt her from her newly planned road. Life had offered an unwelcome detour less than four weeks ago, when her popular café burned to the ground on a windswept October night. She'd watched the flames devour ten years of hard work and sacrifice, everything gone in two short hours. It made her heart ache to think how quickly things could change.

"You're working here, Tina?" Max angled his head slightly, and his appreciative look said this was an interesting—and nice—turn of events.

"Tina came on board to help when I got sick," Charlie explained. He indicated the waterfront southwest of them with a thrust of his chin. "She had the nicest little café right over there in Sol Rigby's old mechanics shop. Put a lot of time and money into that place, a bunch of years. Her coffee shop became one of those places folks love to stop at, but it caught fire a few weeks back. The local volunteers did their best to save it, but the sharp north wind and the fire's head start was too much. So Tina's helping us out while we're waiting for the dust to settle with my treatments."

Concern darkened Max's gaze as he turned her way, as if the loss of her beloved business mattered, as if she mattered.

Don't look like that, Max.

Don't look like you care that my hopes and dreams went up in smoke. That despite how I invested every penny and ounce of energy into building that business, it evaporated in one crazy, flame-filled night. You're not the caring type, remember? When life turns tragic, you tend to disappear. And I've had enough of that to last a lifetime.

Tears pricked her eyes.

She'd been doing better these past few weeks. She could

walk past the burned-out building and not shed a tear. Oh, she shed some mental ones each time, but she hadn't cried for real since that first week, when rain or a puff of wind sent the smell of burned-out wood wafting through the village.

"Tina, I'm so sorry." He looked like he wanted to say more, but stopped himself. He appraised her, then stepped back. "You don't mind teaching me stuff, do you? I'm pretty good with a grappling hook or an all-terrain vehicle on caterpillar treads. Put a semiautomatic in my hands and I'm on my game." He made a G.I. Joe–type motion and stance, ready to stand guard for truth, justice and the American way. "But Dad's new computerized cash registers?" He made a face of fear, and the fact that he steered the conversation away from her pain meant he recognized the emotion and cared.

Sure he cares. Like you're a kid sister who just broke her favorite toy. Get hold of yourself, will you? "I'll be glad to show you whatever you need, Max." She shifted her gaze left. "Charlie, are you staying today?"

"Naw." Frustration marred Charlie's normal smile. "The treatments are catching up with me. When Max showed up at the house yesterday and said he was here to run the store for as long as we need him, well, I'll tell you." Charlie slapped a hand on his youngest son's back. "It was a gift from God. I'd just told Jenny we needed someone here to help you and Earl, with the holidays coming up and all. And while I hate that your pretty little restaurant burned—"

The anxious look in the older man's eyes made Tina recognize a timeline she was loathe to see.

"Having you here, and now Max, well…" Charlie breathed deep. "It's easier for me to focus on getting well, knowing the store is in good hands. I know you're not planning to stay in Kirkwood, Tina, but I thank God every night that we've got you here now. I hate having your mother—" he moved his gaze to Max while Tina fought a new lump of throat-tightening emotion "—worrying over me all the time. But you know her, there's no keeping her from it. And while I'm not one to be fussed over, it's good to have her on my side right now."

Old guilt and his new reality gut-stabbed Max.

Time had gone by. Mistakes had been made. No matter how many battles he fought, no matter how many medals the army pinned on his chest, a part of him couldn't move beyond the teenage boy who'd made a grievous error in judgment years ago.

He swallowed hard but kept his face even. "I should have come back sooner, Dad. I know that. But I'm here now, and I'll do everything I can to make things easier for you and Mom. That's if I can keep my mind on hardware with such pretty help." He slanted a glance of pretended innocence Tina's way.

His ruse of humor worked.

Charlie's laugh lightened the moment. Tina looked like she wanted to mop the floor with him, making jokes at a moment of truth, but Max knew his father. Charlie Campbell would be the first to say that getting crazy emotional over must-have treatments and their outcomes wasn't in anyone's best interests.

You could have come back. You chose not to. That one's all on you, soldier.

Max's heart weighed heavy as Charlie picked up his car keys. Ten years of staying away, grabbing for a future because he couldn't face the past. He'd lost time with his mother, his father, his siblings. Time that could never be regained.

Now he was home, determined to make amends and begin again. Charlie and Jenny Campbell had taken in a five-year-old boy, dumped by his mother the week before Christmas, and brought him to their sprawling lakeside home. They'd changed his life that day, given him a second chance not all children get.

He loved them for it. Now? Time to give back. And if reconnecting with his hometown meant facing old wrongs? Then it was about time he manned up and did just that because staying away hadn't fixed anything. Over the years he'd faced enemies on three separate continents. He could handle Kirkwood Lake.

Once his father left the store, Max turned toward Tina.

"Don't you dare break their hearts again, Max Campbell."

He'd come home expecting emotional shrapnel.

Tina's flat-out decree was more like a direct hit at close range. He started to speak, but Tina moved a half step forward, invading his space. "What were you thinking disappearing like that? All those years gone. What were you doing all that time?"

"My job?" He let his inflection say the answer was obvious, but he knew Tina was right. He could have come back. Should have come back. He'd missed weddings, baptisms, anniversaries and holidays. And he'd done it on purpose, because it was easier to face current danger than past lapses in judgment. He got careless and stupid, but he didn't need this drop-dead gorgeous gray-eyed beauty to ream him out over it.

Although he preferred her sass to the tears she'd been fighting minutes before. Tears went hand in hand with high drama. If there was something Max steered clear of, it was high-drama women.

"Your job wasn't 24/7/365." She folded her hands across

her chest, leveled him a look and didn't seem at all fazed that he had her by a good seven inches and sixty pounds. Or that he was a munitions expert. Her bravado made him smile inside, but he held back, knowing she wouldn't appreciate his amusement.

"I should have come back. Phone calls weren't enough. I know that now." He'd known it then, too, but it had been easier to stay away. Still, this was *his* personal business, not hers. Fortunately his straightforward admission helped take the wind out of her sails.

Good. He had no intention of being yelled at all day. With the high-volume sales of winter and holiday items upon them, he knew Campbell's Hardware would be cranking. His job was to learn the new aspects of an old business ASAP, shouldering the work his parents did so naturally. "For the moment, if you can take a break from yelling at me, I need to learn as much as I can as quickly as I can to help out. Now we either do this together—" he mimicked her stance and saw her wince as if recognizing her stubbornness "—or we work as separate entities. But, Tina?" He held her gaze, waiting until she blinked in concession to continue.

Only she didn't.

He shrugged that off mentally and stood his ground. "We've got to take care of this for Dad's sake. And Mom's. No matter how you might feel about me. Which means we might have to declare a truce, at least during working hours. Agreed?"

Her expression softened. She stared over his shoulder, sighed, then brought her eyes back to his. "Agreed."

He refused to acknowledge her reluctance. Ten years in the service taught him to pick his battles. He'd seen her face when they'd talked of her business burning. He understood that working side by side with the Campbell prodigal probably hadn't made her short list, and life had done a number on her.

But when she took a deep breath and stuck out her hand again, he realized that Tina Martinelli was made of pretty strong stuff. "Do-over," she instructed.

He smiled, nodded and accepted her hand in his.

"Max, you might not remember me. I'm Tina Martinelli and I'm here to help your parents."

He should resist. He knew it, knew it the minute her eyes locked with his. Held.

But he couldn't and so he gave her hand a light squeeze and smiled. "Well, Tina, I do remember you, but what I remember is a pesky tomboy who whistled louder, ran faster and jumped higher than most of the guys around."

The blush heightened again. Was it because he remembered or because he'd brought up her penchant for sports and winning? Max wasn't sure, but he leaned closer, just enough to punctuate his meaning. "This Tina?" He shook his head, dropped her hand and stepped back. He didn't give her a once-over because he didn't have to. Her face said she understood. "This Tina is a surprise and I can't say I'm sorry to be working with her. Reason enough to clean up and hurry into work each morning."

"Which means we need to set ground rules." She glossed over his compliment as if it hadn't affected her. Max allotted her extra points for that and played along. "Employees are not allowed to fraternize outside of work."

Max frowned. "My parents own this place and I'm going to guarantee they fraternize outside of work. That's how they got to be parents."

She bristled, looking really cute as she did. But he couldn't think of that. There was work to be done so he held up a hand. "You're right. I know you and Earl have been picking up a lot of slack, so my goal is to help you any way I can. If we can keep Mom and Dad from worrying about the store, Dad can focus on getting through his treatments. Getting well."

"Then we share the same objective. Perfect." She gave him a crisp nod as she moved to a stack of holiday-themed boxes. "As long as we keep our focus on that, we shouldn't have any problems."

Saucy and determined, the grown-up Tina wasn't much different than she'd been years ago. He knew he should stop. Let her have the last word. But when she slanted a "keep your distance" look over her shoulder, he couldn't resist. "Working for the government taught me to get around problems efficiently, Tina Martinelli. I expect that might come in handy now and then."

Come in handy?

Not with her, it wouldn't.

Oh, she saw the charm and self-assuredness that had drawn girls to Max back in their youth. Refined now, the charisma was more dangerous, almost volatile. But Tina hadn't spent the last decade pining for her childhood crush. She'd managed to have her heart broken twice since, so Max could flirt and tempt all he wanted. It would do him no good.

Tina was immune.

You want to be immune, but face it, darling. Damp palms say something else entirely.

She shushed the internal warning, but when she leaned in to show Max how to engage cash register functions, the scent of him made her long to draw closer.

She didn't. She ignored the fact that he smelled of sandalwood and soap and total guy, and that the flash of his smile brightened a room.

She didn't need any rooms brightened, thank you. A few LED lightbulbs took care of that in a cost-effective way.

Over the years, she'd shrugged off her teenage attraction to Max as silly adolescent stuff. But today, seeing the straightforward warmth of the hardened but humorous man he'd become?

That might be tough to resist.

Fortunately Tina wasn't in the market for anything in Kirkwood Lake these days. Least of all another broken heart. Been there, done that. Overrated.

She showed him through the layout of the store. His parents had done a complete remodel four years previous, making Max's memories obsolete, and the first thing he noted out loud were the rotational seasonal displays set at four separate locations. "I expect this was my mother's idea."

Tina nodded as she unlocked the front door and officially opened the story for business. "She likes to go to regional conferences that teach how to build sales while keeping overhead in check."

"Always a trick in retail." Max nodded to the first customer in the door, a woman, carrying an older-model chain saw that had seen better days.

"Is Earl here yet?" The look she gave Tina and Max said she didn't put much trust in their abilities.

"No, ma'am," Max told her. "Not 'til noon. But maybe I can help?"

She looked at him, really looked, then formed her mouth into a grim line. "Maxwell Campbell, I do believe you still owe me for some flowers that went missing from my garden about twelve years back. Give or take a summer or two."

Max's grimace said his memory clicked to a younger version of the woman before him. "You're absolutely correct, Mrs. Hyatt. Those would be red roses and I believe they found their way over to Sophie Benedict's house. I'll be happy to make that up to you now with my apologies for the delay. And ask your forgiveness, of course."

The look she settled on him said maybe that was okay, and maybe it wasn't. "How long have you served our country, young man?"

"Over a decade."

Her mouth softened. Her shoulders relaxed. "I'd say we're more than even." She clapped a hand to his shoulder, hometown pride showing in her eyes, her smile. "Welcome home, Max. I expect your parents are most pleased to have you here, and just in time to share the holidays together."

"Yes, ma'am. My mom goes a little bit crazy over Thanksgiving and Christmas, that's for sure. And about that saw?" He dropped his gaze to the chain saw in her arms.

Her face said she was inclined to wait until Earl's arrival nearly three hours later.

"If you bring it to Dad's tool bench, I'd be glad to have a look."

"If you think you can." She didn't try to mask the dubious note in her voice. "It's been a long time since you've worked with your dad."

"True." He led the way to Charlie's well-lit bench and table at the back corner, a popular gathering place for small-town talk and broken tools. "But I remember a thing or two. And working for Uncle Sam taught me a few new tricks. Let's see what's going on." He examined the pieces, then nodded. "We've got a bad clutch. Tina, does Dad carry parts for all models in the back or just current ones?"

His quiet confidence in his abilities lightened Tina's angst. Working for the Campbells helped them and her, but with Charlie out of commission and Earl on limited hours, she'd been fielding a lot of questions with few answers the past two weeks. Maybe having Max around wouldn't be so bad, not if he could actually make sense out of the more difficult hardware inquiries. "I'll check and see. If we have to order it, we won't get it until next Tuesday, Mrs. Hyatt. Is that all right?"

"Tuesday's fine with me. Then would you be able to fix it right away?" she wondered. She hesitated, looking a little uncomfortable, then explained, "I hate to push, knowing what's going on with your dad and all, but I promised my husband I'd get this fixed before wood-cutting season. Once the cold hits, he'll take to the woods for next year's heating supply, but he can't cut without his saw. And with the Festival of Lights coming up, I'm going to have my hands full. I expect you're taking that over for your father, as well?"

Max sent a blank look from her to Tina and back. "Festival of Lights? I'm not following you."

"The annual Christmas lighting event we've been doing for years," Mrs. Hyatt replied. "This year it's the final big event of our bicentennial celebration," she continued. "Your dad heads up the committee, we use the funds raised from the park drive-through to support the women's shelter in Clearwater, and Tina and I handle the food venues with a bunch of volunteers. That money helps stock food pantries all year long. Joe Burns is helping." She ticked off her fingers, listing familiar names. "The Radcliffes, Sawyers and Morgans are all on board, as well. We've got everything planned out, of course, because it starts soon, but no one knows how to do lighting grids as well as Charlie Campbell."

One phrase stood out.

The Sawyers. Pete's family, Tina's neighbors on Upper

Lake Road. Pete used to love ditching both his little sister, Sherrie, and Tina. He and Max would take their small boat out and go fishing or girl-watching. When they were young, fishing took precedence. By the time they finished high school?

Partying had replaced fishing for Pete.

Regret speared Max. He shelved it purposely. He'd come back to help and make amends. Right now, helping took precedence, even if it meant coming face-to-face with Pete's family sooner rather than later.

Business owners were taking advantage of today's nice weather to hang festive garland. Town crews had manned a cherry-picker truck to string lights through Main Street trees, and decorated wreaths marked each old-fashioned light pole. Like it or not they were two weeks shy of Thanksgiving and the town was knee-deep in a project that depended on Charlie's calm help and expertise.

"I'll talk to my dad and see what I can do to help. We'll cover it, Mrs. Hyatt. No worries."

Her sigh of relief said he'd answered correctly. "And you're okay with me coming by next Wednesday to pick up the saw?"

"I'll put the part in as soon as it arrives," Max promised. "If there's any delay, we'll give you a call."

"That would be wonderful." She watched as he filled out a tag with her name, gave him her phone number, then smiled, more relaxed than when she came into the store. "I expect you'll both be at the final committee meeting Wednesday night?"

Special ops had prepared Max to tack with the prevailing wind, no matter what the mission. "Absolutely. When and where?"

"We used to have them at my café." The resignation in Tina's tone said her loss rubbed raw. "But Carmen Bianchi said we could meet in her apartment behind Vintage Place instead. Seven o'clock."

"I'll be there," Max promised. "And we'll be ready to implement Dad's action plan, Mrs. Hyatt."

"Good!" Her smile said his confidence appeased her concerns. Which meant he hadn't lost his touch, but if he was coming face-to-face with the Sawyers in a few days, and expected to run this light show thing, he needed to get his mental ducks in a row. Fast.

Max watched Mrs. Hyatt walk out the door, then took the broken saw to the second bench. "I know Dad always puts them in back in the order they come in, but I don't want to forget my promise to her."

"Seeing it is a good reminder," Tina replied. "And the back room is kind of crowded right now anyway." She greeted someone, then waved another pair of customers upstairs to the "country store" shop, another one of his mother's ideas. Fifteen years ago, folks had kind of ridiculed the idea of a home shop in a hardware store, but no one scoffed now. Campbell's "Country Cove" on the second floor did enough winter business to pay the bills and record a profit, a huge plus in northern towns.

When Tina came back to the front, Max indicated the door and Mrs. Hyatt's retreating back with a quick glance. "What have you been doing the past few weeks when customers like that came in? Did you send them elsewhere?"

"Come with me." Tina led him into the back room, threaded a path through the overstock and the glass-cutting corner, then waved toward Charlie's equipment fix-it zone for larger repairs. "This is what Earl's been working on this past week when he was healthy enough to be here."

Max counted eighteen separate tools in various stages of repair. "Are these due to be picked up soon?"

"Tomorrow. That's our regular tool pickup day now."

Tomorrow. Of course Earl was scheduled to work a one-to-five shift today, but that was a lot of fixing to do before they opened tomorrow morning. "Are the necessary parts available? Have they been delivered?"

"With the exception of Herb Langdon's snowblower, yes. And I called and told him the part was on back order. Earl was out sick this week so all this stuff is here, waiting. Tomorrow morning we'll have a bunch of people coming in to pick up tools that most likely won't be ready."

"So that's why my mother came in yesterday." Max made a face of realization. "Earl was sick."

"And you know your mother. She said it was fine because your brothers took care of keeping Charlie company while she was here, but I could tell she was torn."

"Luke and Seth aren't exactly nursing material." Max respected his older brothers, two decorated county sheriff's deputies, but nursing care wasn't their forte.

"He needs company more than care right now," Tina answered. "And your mom needs to get out now and again. Catch her breath. You know."

Max didn't know any such thing. His mother was the most dedicated and loving person he'd ever met. The thought of her wanting to leave Charlie's side seemed alien. "I expect she'd rather be with Dad. Just in case."

The uncertainty in Tina's expression said he might know tools but he'd just flunked Women 101. And that was somewhat surprising, because Max thought he knew women fairly well. But maybe not Kirkwood Lake women.

Despite Earl's help that afternoon, by the time they locked the doors at five o'clock, there were still three lawn mowers, two leaf blowers, two power-washers and two log-splitters awaiting repair.

Earl held his knit cap in his hand, sheepish. "I shoulda knowed I wasn't gonna get to all those with Charlie gone,

Max. I can come in early tomorrow and help." He slapped a hand to his head, then shook his head. "No, I'm wrong, Mavis is havin' some eye thing done tomorrow mornin' and I promised to drive her. If she breaks the appointment who knows how long it will take to get another. And she'd have my head for puttin' her off."

"Oh, those women," Tina muttered, just out of Earl's range of hearing.

Max fought a smile and sent Earl off. "I'll stay late, see what I can do. Thanks for today, though, Earl. It was great working with you."

"Same here." Earl made his way to the door, paused, thought, then continued as if he'd never stopped at all. Tina watched him go before she faced Max.

"Do you want me to stay and help? If you show me what to do, I might be able to take some of the pressure off you."

Assessing the number of tools and the variety of fixes, Max wished that were true, but— "It would take me longer to train you tonight than it would to fix them myself, but I appreciate the offer, Tina. And working with Earl today gave me a refresher course in small-engine repair." He pointed to a stack of thin books alongside the bench. "I've got manuals for each of the models from the internet." He shrugged, pulled on one of his dad's sweatshirts from the rack behind the workroom bench and waved her on. "I'll be fine. Not like I haven't pulled double duty in my time."

"If you're sure?"

"I am. I'll call Mom, tell her I'm running late. It's all good."

"All right. I'll open in the morning, so if you need to sleep in, go ahead. I'll have things covered."

"Thanks. I just might do that." He wouldn't, but he appreciated the offer, just the same. In fact, looking at the work spread out before him, he wasn't sure he'd make it home at all, but that was okay. Jenny and Charlie Campbell had rocked him to sleep at night, held him through a phase of unrelenting nightmares and ran him from town to town as he tore up soccer fields across the county. Staying up late to help them out?

Not a big deal at all.

Chapter Two

Tina grabbed the hardware store door handle Monday morning, emotionally sorting through the scene she had just passed. A crew of uniformed firemen, sifting through the remains of her café, searching for evidence of arson. Tina shivered at the thought that anyone would deliberately burn a building, risk harming others and destroy property.

It couldn't be true. Mild crime was unusual here in Kirkwood Lake. Felony crimes like arson? Assault?

Virtually unheard of.

The door swung open beneath her grip, and she stepped in cautiously, looking left and right. Had Max forgotten to lock up? That seemed unlikely for a guy who made his living completing surreptitious missions, but—

"Tina, is that you? I've got coffee back here. Come get some. If you drink coffee, that is."

"I owned a café. I live on coffee. Gimme." She reached for the cup as she entered the back room, then stopped, surprised. "Max. They're all done. Every last one."

The array of broken equipment had been put back together, each one tagged with the owner's name and the cost of repair. They formed a pretty line along Charlie's back-room bench, then marched across the work floor, ready to be loaded into vehicles from the rear loading dock. There would be no reckoning with angry customers, no putting folks off, no begging for more time, hoping people understood business limitations brought on by Charlie's illness. "I can't believe this." Tina turned in a full circle, then stopped when she faced Max again. "You stayed all night."

"Not the first time I've stayed late somewhere. Won't be the last." He brushed off the sacrifice like it was no big deal, and that almost made her like him. She'd had enough of guys who promised one thing, then did another. Max's casual treatment of his sacrifice for his family touched too many of those empty-promise buttons. He directed his attention to the coffee cup. "I wasn't sure what you like, so I got flavored creamers and regular. And sugar. And artificial sugar."

"Covering all the bases." The fact that he'd gone the distance for his parents surprised her. And that he'd provided for her despite his lack of sleep? Downright sweet of him. "Max, this is so nice. Thank you."

"You're welcome."

He hesitated a moment, coffee in hand, as if wanting to say something. Tina prodded him as she stirred hazelnut creamer into her cup. "And?"

His next words surprised her. Because it was old news or because the sympathy in Max's voice rang with quiet sincerity? Maybe both.

"I didn't realize your parents were gone, Tina." His gaze showed regret. "I'm truly sorry."

Max's years away had wrought lots of local change. Losing her parents had become a big part of that "new normal." She sighed. "Me, too."

"And your aunt owns The Pelican's Nest now?" He sipped his coffee and shifted his attention to the east window. The steep peak of the restaurant profile was just visible beyond the parking lot. "I would have thought they'd leave it to you. Or give it to you. Something for all those years of work you put in."

"Well. They didn't."

"Because?"

She didn't want to talk about this. She didn't want to re-hash old Martinelli news the whole town already knew. But Tina knew if she didn't answer, he'd just ask his parents. It wasn't like anything stayed a secret in a small town. "My aunt and uncle were in a position to buy in. They promised to let me manage the business. My father had developed a bad heart, a combination of genetics and smoking, and he needed to step down. Mom and Dad moved to Florida to escape the tough winters and my uncle booted me to the curb."

"He fired you?"

"Yes."

"Oh, man."

He was feeling sorry for her, and the expression on his face said he couldn't understand family acting like that, treating each other that way. Well.

Neither could she. "It was a long time ago."

"Yes. But then you opened a café there." He indicated the burned-out shell visible through the west-facing window. "With their restaurant right here." He turned back toward the window facing the parking lot and whistled lightly. "Gutsy."

Tina made a face. "Gutsy, yes. And maybe a little mean."

"Mean?" He put away a handful of small tools as he scrunched his forehead. "How can that be mean?"

"Because as my business grew, their customers dwindled," Tina admitted. "And that made my uncle grumpier than usual, and he was pretty miserable already. That couldn't have been fun for Aunt Laura and Ryan."

He raised one absolutely gorgeous brow at the mention of her cousin's name.

"My cousin. Their only child. And now my uncle's dead, my aunt's running the place on her own with half the help she needs, and raising a kid who's hanging with a rough bunch from Clearwater. So maybe if I hadn't been bullheaded and put my café right under their noses…"

"Where your success would be painfully obvious…"

She frowned. "Exactly. Maybe things would be different. Maybe we could actually be like a normal family. Like yours."

"Ah."

"You have so much to be grateful for, Max."

His face said he knew that.

"So staying away, leaving your parents and brothers and sisters, shrugging them all off…" She set her coffee cup down and faced him. "I don't get it. I'd give anything to have a family. My parents are gone, my mom died two years after my dad, I've got no brothers or sisters, and my one aunt won't acknowledge me if we pass on the street. I'd trade places with you in a heartbeat."

Sympathy deepened his expression. "You know, I never thought of family in terms of temporary until Mom called me with Dad's prognosis. Reality smacked me upside the head and said *head home, soldier*. But you're right, Tina. I've got a lot to make up for, but standing and talking won't do anything but put me to sleep this morning. I'm going to pull the last of those Christmas displays out of the shed and bring them in. I promised Mom we'd get them into place today."

He wanted a change of subject. So did she. She turned, flipped the Closed sign to Open and turned the key in the door. "Bring 'em in, Max. I'll be happy to help."

"Thank you, Tina. I'd appreciate it."

He was playing nice

His generosity rankled Tina more. After seeing investigators comb through the cold morning rubble of her beloved business, discussing her family's casual disregard for each other was more unwelcome than usual. But Max would know nothing about that, because Campbells looked out for one another.

She took care of a handful of customers while Max built a Christmas lights display case in their seasonal corner. Once he had it firmly in place, she helped stock the wide range of holiday lighting kits.

"Doesn't it seem early to be putting out Christmas stuff?"

Tina gaped at him, then laughed. "You've been in the army too long. The stores start shelving Christmas items as soon as their back-to-school displays are depleted. By mid-September, most places are stocked, lit up and ready to roll with holiday sales."

"And Thanksgiving gets lost in the shuffle." Max's lament surprised her, because it was a feeling they shared.

"I love Thanksgiving," she admitted. "I love the simplicity, the warmth, the food. Of course, I'm Italian, why wouldn't I love the food?" The look she sent him made him smile, but his grin turned to understanding when she added, "The whole idea of an entire country, praying their thanks to God, regardless of faith. I just love it."

"You know, it's funny." Max eased a hip onto the sales counter as he grabbed a bottle of water. "When you're in the field on holidays, most of the guys seem to feel the loss of Thanksgiving more than any other."

"More than Christmas?"

"Yeah. I might be wrong." He shrugged, thinking. "Most soldiers get stuff at Christmas. Even the ones who don't have family are hooked up with agencies that send care packages to deployed soldiers. But on Thanksgiving, there's nothing but memories of what was. What could have been. What might be again. *If* you make it back.

Maybe it was just me." He stood, stretched and tossed his bottle into the recycling tote. "But I don't think so."

She'd never thought of it that way. She'd helped on Wounded Warrior projects, she'd arranged pickups for the Vietnam Veterans thrift shops, but she'd never thought about how lonely Thanksgiving must be when you're thousands of miles away from anything American. "Hey, if you need to catch some sleep, head home. I've got this. Earl will be here in an hour and we'll be all set."

"I'll leave once Earl's here," Max answered. He rolled his shoulders, stretched once more, and she did her best to ignore the amazing muscle definition formed by long years in the armed services. He moved to the front of the store. "I'm going to use the Cat to level the parking-lot stone. I can see where the water's been puddling, and that won't get any better once the snow hits."

"Good."

"And when I come back in, can you give me the low-down on this festival thing we talked about yesterday? There's not much time left, and I work better with a plan in my head."

"From the looks of that back room, you do pretty well without a plan, too." She didn't say how she'd dreaded facing disappointed customers today, their expected equipment lying unfixed in the back room.

He shot her a grin over his shoulder. "Let's see if they work before giving me too much credit."

"You tested them, right?"

He ignored her question and kept on walking. Was he laughing? At her?

She finished the Christmas lights display as a customer arrived to pick up one of the newly fixed lawn mowers. When they wheeled their repaired machine out the back door, she felt a stab of pride. It might not be a big deal that Chuck Beadle was going to be able to give his yard a last mowing it didn't really need, but it was important that their efforts to maintain Charlie and Jenny's business as he fought his battle with cancer were successful. And without Max, it wouldn't have happened, so she needed to give credit where credit was due.

Her cell phone signaled an incoming call. She pulled it out, saw the realty office number and picked up quickly. "Myra, good morning."

"Hey, good morning to you, Tina! I'm emailing you a short list of potential sites for your café if you're still thinking of Spencerport as your go-to place."

"I am," she replied. "That or Brockport." She'd done her homework and these Erie Canal locations in Western New York had lots of potential. "They both have proximity to the expressway, and they're on main-feeder corridor to other towns. What I want is a west-side-of-the-road location and a drive-through for those a.m. customers."

"Did you have a drive-through in Kirkwood?" Myra asked.

"I was lakefront, so no, I didn't. And we're a destination spot, not a commuter town, so it's a different configuration."

"Won't you miss the water?"

Miss the water?

Yeah, absolutely. But if she wasn't willing to sacrifice something to change things up, nothing would ever happen, and that option didn't cut it anymore. The time for change was here. Now. "Not if I have a view of the canal," she promised. "Or at least proximity to it so folks can grab a cuppa, head for the canal walkway and stroll along the banks watching the boats. Those villages are a walker's dream, so no. I won't miss the water."

It was an outright lie. She knew it, and she was pretty

sure Myra's silence said she recognized Tina's resignation, but was kind enough not to call her on it.

Tina loved the water. She loved taking her little boat out on calm summer days. Dropping a line just off the docks outside the Kirkwood Lodge where perch and bass gathered in the heat of summer. She'd caught her share of fish that way, a sweet respite from work. Private time, time to think. And pray. And dream.

But her dreams were gone now. Ruined.

She promised Myra she'd look at the property listings in the email and get back to her. Another customer walked in, then another, and pretty soon she was too busy to think about smoldering dreams and ruined hopes. She'd promised herself she'd never get mired in the past again. She meant to keep that promise.

"I brought Beezer in to keep you company," Jenny Campbell announced as she came through the back door of the shop a little later. "And I'm going to drag Max home to catch some sleep. I think that's a good trade, don't you, Tina?"

"Leave the dog and take Max?" Tina sent Max a look that said she approved fully. "I think I'm getting the better end of this deal."

"Hey, Beeze." As Tina moved their way, Max squatted low and gave the aging golden retriever a long belly rub the dog loved. "You missing the action, old boy?"

"He is." Jenny tipped a mock frown down to the beloved pet. "I reminded him that his master is sick and good dogs stay by their master's side."

"They do in books," Tina agreed. "But Beeze was raised in town. He likes to check out the hustle and bustle of the shop."

"He's restless if he's home too much," Jenny admitted. "When I let him out, he starts prowling the yard as if looking for a way down to the village. I'm afraid he'll wander close to the road and won't hear a car coming around the bend."

"Well, he can keep an eye on Tina if I'm heading home." Max grabbed his bomber jacket from the back hook as Earl finished up with a customer. The thought of a few hours of sleep sounded real good now. "You guys will be okay?"

"Tina will boss me around, and I'll answer any fix-it questions that arise." Earl's wry tone said he was only partially kidding. "Same old, same old."

"Women are bossy creatures." Max smiled at the older man, then turned his attention to Tina. "We never did talk about the festival thing. My bad. It got busy and—"

"Max, we can't expect you to do the festival, too." Jenny frowned as she caught the gist of the conversation. "That's not fair. You came home to have time with Dad. If we keep you working day and night, then—"

"We'll make time for both, I promise. I managed to run a unit with a lot of guys and barely got my hands dirty, Mom. I'm good at delegating. But first I need to know what's going on." He turned back to Tina. "I don't suppose you have time to come over tonight and go over things? That way we could have Mom and Dad's input, too."

"You can have supper with us." Jenny's face said inviting Tina to supper made everything better. Max wasn't so sure Tina would agree now that he was on hand, but she'd been civil all day, and that was a sweet improvement. Of course they'd been busy from the moment they unlocked the doors, so maybe the key to keeping Tina happy was keeping her busy.

"I'll come over once we close up," Tina promised. "And I'll bring Beeze along. That way he's got the best of both worlds."

"Thank you, Tina." When Jenny gave Tina a big old hug, Max realized their relationship had grown close over his years away. His mother's next words confirmed it.

"I don't know what we'd do without you." Jenny's voice stopped short of saying she wanted Tina to stay right here in Kirkwood, but the inflection was clear.

Tina winked as she headed for the register area. "Back at ya. Gotta go. Mrs. Lana is here for her leaf blower, and last night's killing frost means she'll be really glad to have it back, especially with snow in the late-week forecast."

"I love this." Max stopped at the back door and swept the town center a long, slow look of appreciation. "The old town buildings. The lake. The decorations that look like an old New England village. Now that I'm home and see it all again, I realize how much I missed it."

Jenny looped her arm through his as they went through the back doorway. "Always something to miss, no matter where we are. But I'm glad you're here, that I don't have to run down the coast to see you. As fun as that is, I prefer having you home for a while. And I'm making your favorite dinner, so once you've gotten some sleep, I intend to fatten you up."

"A mother's prerogative." Max yawned as he moved toward his upgraded sports car. "It feels good to be home."

Tina watched him pull away from inside the store.

He drove a muscle car, a total chick magnet. He flashed those big brown eyes and that smile like it was nothing, nothing at all. And every now and again he'd watch her, as if appraising.

Was he comparing the old her with the new?

And if so, what did he see? And why did it matter to her?

Sherrie Morgan breezed through the front door a few minutes later. "The promised cold snap has arrived," she noted as the screen door bumped shut behind her. "And tell me if the 4-1-1 is right. Max Campbell is back and un-attached? Girlfriend, this is not news anyone should keep to themselves unless, of course, one really, truly wants to keep it to herself?"

Tina retrieved the last repaired lawn mower and cautioned Sherrie with a look. "He is back, yes, to help his parents. Sherrie, come on, you know the situation. They're delighted to have him here and I'm pleased to have someone with hardware knowledge on hand. I was totally in over my head last week. But you know Max as well as anyone. Here today, gone tomorrow."

"Oh. Ouch. Unfair." Sherrie picked out three boxes of Christmas lights, paused, then added a fourth to her stack. "He was eighteen," Sherrie reminded her. "And people react to sadness differently. I think back to that day, losing Pete and Amy, and for years I kept wondering what I could have done differently. If I'd been less pesky, less bothersome, would they have stayed at home? Hung out by the campfire? Maybe knowing there'd be a kid sister around later pushed them to take the boat out. Have some romantic boyfriend/girlfriend time."

"Sherrie—"

"I know it wasn't my fault." Sherrie brushed off Tina's protest with a shrug. "I'm all grown up now, I know people make choices every day, and that I was just a normal kid, pestering her big brother and wishing I was as pretty as Amy with her long blond hair and those big blue eyes. And then they were gone, and it left such a hole. But just because Max didn't come around doesn't make him a bad person, Tina. He might have been older than us, but he was still a kid who'd just lost his best friend. And that couldn't have been easy."

Sherrie's argument made perfect sense, but Sherrie

hadn't done a decade-long disappearing act after college. Max had. And Tina was done with capricious men, even if her heart managed to skip a beat every time Max walked into a room. Clearly hearts knew nothing and were not to be trusted. End of story.

"So you're working together." Sherrie ended the sentence on a note of question, hunting for an informational update. Tina gave her a look that said nothing interesting was happening. Or would happen.

"Of necessity. Jenny and Charlie need help. Max and I are available. Simple math, one plus one and all that."

"Except you had a crush on him all through high school," Sherrie mused as she pulled out her debit card. "Honey, when God plants your dream right in front of you, I think it's an invitation to grab hold. See where life leads."

"I know exactly where my life is heading, thanks." Tina patted the thin stack of computer printouts. "These are possible café sites near the Erie Canal. Not so far away that I can't visit, but far enough to wipe the slate clean, Sherrie. And that's something I desperately need. A new beginning, a fresh start."

"And you've prayed about this, chatted it up with God, right?"

"I think the fire was a good sign that my time in Kirkwood has come to a close," Tina told her while ignoring the fact she'd done no such thing. A thin ribbon of guilt tweaked her. "If you're looking for signs, that one was pretty direct."

Sherrie tucked her debit card back into her purse once Tina ran it through, but refused to be dissuaded. "If someone did set that fire, that's no message from God, Tina. That's a depraved act of humanity and shouldn't go unpunished. And folks around here rebuild after disaster all the time. Look what happened after the floods last year. And those blizzards that took out three old barns? We're re-builders. We don't give up. And I don't even want to think about you being more than two hours away. We've been besties forever, so yes, selfishly, I want you here when my baby comes. Babies should have their godmothers close by, don't you think?"

"You're pregnant?" Delight coursed through Tina. Sherrie and her husband had been hoping for a child for years. With two sad outcomes behind them, a well-set pregnancy seemed almost impossible. But a tiny prick of envy niggled the rise of joy, because Tina had thought her life would be on a similar track by now. Married. A cute kid or two. Maybe a dog like Beezer, loving and easygoing. Surging happiness displaced the twinge of envy, and she grabbed her best friend in a big hug. "Tell me when."

"In less than five months," Sherrie said. "We kept it quiet until we were far enough along to be more confident, so in four and a half months, I'll need your help. But you can't help me if you're so far away."

Sherrie was right. She'd be little help from that distance, and starting a new business took a level of dedication that went beyond the norm. She remembered her early days with the café, long, tedious days, keeping overhead down while working to build business up. That meant lots of personal man-hours.

Was she ready to do that again?

The morning's image cropped up once more, the firemen, sifting through the ashes, their movements kicking up the smell of old, wet, burned wood, a hunk of ugly set in the middle of the season of light.

What if this person was targeting her personally?

She knew the investigators were checking out Sol Rigby to see if he had a reason to torch his own place, but Tina doubted that. Sol was frugal, and he didn't look well-off, but Tina was pretty sure the old guy was doing okay financially. Which meant he had no reason to want insurance money.

The realization that they would investigate her hit hard. They would check her financials, and while not great, they weren't bad, either. And no way would she do such a thing.

But clearly the investigators thought someone had purposely burned down her place. The question was who? And why?

"I know the arson investigators talked to your aunt today. And I know this because Jim was with them," Sherrie offered as if she'd read where her thoughts had wandered. "He didn't repeat anything that was said, but he said it was a tough interview."

"My café hurt her business."

Sherrie nodded. "Which might be motive enough to get it out of the way."

"Aunt Laura would never do that. Rocco, maybe." Memories of her uncle's temperamental tirades hit hard, but Rocco was gone, and Laura wasn't the hurtful type. She was more mouse than lion and Rocco had taken advantage of that for years. "I know they're in a tight spot. Rocco didn't believe in life insurance so Laura and Ryan got left with nothing but a failing business and a stack of bills."

"Well, he wasn't the sort to look out for his family," Sherrie replied. "Which means Laura's trying to run the place alone because Ryan is no help. Jim said that bunch of boys from Clearwater are a tough group. They're old enough to drive and he's sneaking out to hang out with them. Laura's so busy trying to do things on her own, no one's watching the kid. And that means trouble's on the way."

Talking about this made Tina tired. She'd run the scenario through her head countless times, and had come up

with nothing good. All the more reason to start anew somewhere else. She hated drama and avoided it at all costs,
but burned-out businesses came with their own spectacle
of tragedy.

"Right now let's focus on this baby. Do we know if it's
a boy or a girl?"

"A boy." Sheer delight said Sherrie was more than
okay with the change of subject. "We found out today.
Jim wanted to be surprised, but I said uh-uh. I wanted to
know so I can give him the coolest little kid bedroom ever."

"And Jim said, 'Whatever you want, honey.'"

"Exactly!" Sherrie laughed and moved outside where
Earl was loading the snowblower into the back of her pickup
truck. "We'll talk soon. Don't make any rash moves, okay?"

"I won't. I promise."

"See you later."

Excitement colored everything about Sherrie today. Her
tone, her face, her eyes. And Tina was overjoyed for her
friend. She understood the struggles Sherrie had faced,
and now she'd pray for a happy ending, a beautiful healthy
baby boy for Sherrie and Jim to hold and feed and do all
that other stuff one must do with babies.

She and Sherrie had grown up together. Their family homes had been right next to each other. They'd shared
classes together, dance instructors and soccer teams. She'd
been Sherrie's maid of honor five years ago, and Sherrie had
a rose chiffon bridesmaid dress collecting dust in her closet
from Tina's short-lived engagement a few years after that.
Evan Veltre had decided tall, buxom and raven-haired was
more his style. Dumping her mid-engagement made her previ-
ous boyfriend's infidelity seem mild by comparison. At least
they hadn't been engaged when the blonde caught his eye.

A niggle of sensibility tweaked her.

Had she been hurrying the process, wanting to fall in

love? Had she been trying to fit the guy, rather than letting God's timing take charge?

The pinch of common sense was nudged by a twinge of guilt. She did like to make her own path, chart her own course, a charge-ahead kind of woman in many ways. Sherrie had asked if she'd turned to prayer.

She hadn't, not really. Was she too busy, too independent to trust God?

Beezer whined and pawed the door, ready to go. Tina drew a breath, switched off the lights, activated the alarm and went out the door with the big, gold dog ambling alongside her.

Wind tunneled down Main Street, tumbling the last of autumn's leaves. They scurried along the street, pushed by the stiff breeze, gathering in curves and hollows.

Soon it would snow. And they'd continue to decorate the town in beautiful light, a beacon of Christmas hope and cheer. And once again she'd spend Christmas alone, no family, no beloved, no kids.

Beezer pushed his head up under her arm.

He wanted her to pet him. Talk to him. So she did just that on the drive to the Campbell house, happy that no one could see her talking with the big yellow dog, but more glad of his trusting company.

If nothing else crazy occurred in her life this year, she was determined to get herself a dog. Maybe.

Beezer yipped softly, as if telling her she didn't need another dog, she could still share him. If she stayed.

And there was the crux of the problem. A big part of Tina didn't want to stay and face past failures anymore.

Chapter Three

"Hey, Beeze." Max swung down from the elevated boathouse as Tina rounded the corner of the Campbell house at half past six. He looked sports-channel-commercial-friendly in easy-cut jeans and a long-sleeved Pittsburgh Pirates sweatshirt.

"Did you keep an eye on things, old fella?" He stooped and ruffled the dog's neck, rubbing Beeze's favorite spot beneath the wide collar. "All good?" He looked up at her as he asked the question, and the sight of him, caring for the aging dog, looking all sweet and concerned and amazingly good-looking...

She took three seconds to put her heart back in normal sinus rhythm mode. "Everything went fine. Dozens of happy customers picking up their tools and buying fixer-upper stuff to get ready for the holidays." She frowned as Beeze headed for the water, though she knew she had nothing to worry about. Beeze was a country dog and his daily swim was an old habit now. "He'll smell like wet dog all night."

"I'll put him on the porch. Dad's gotten sensitive to smells. The chemo, I guess. He says nothing smells right anymore."

"Will it get better when he's done?"

Max's expression said he wasn't sure anything would get better, ever. Seeing that, her heart softened more.

"Hope so." Max headed for the house. "Come on in. Beeze will join us once he's done with his swim."

Tina knew that. She'd spent an increasing amount of time at the Campbell house over the past decade. Charlie and Jen were good at taking in strays, and when her family had fallen apart, they'd jumped right in. She'd spent holidays here, preserved food with Jenny during the summer, and when Seth Campbell spotted her café on fire a few weeks back from his house across the road, he'd called 9-1-1 and his parents.

They'd helped her then.

She'd help them now. And she'd have done it for no pay, but Charlie wouldn't hear of it. A true fatherly type, he understood cash was finite in a week-to-week existence, and he insisted on paying her for her time. "You know, if you're too tired, we can go over this stuff in the morning. I know you've had a long day."

"Except we could really use the light guy's take on all this." Max's nod toward the door said Charlie's input was key.

"Is he up to it?"

"Let's ask him." Max swung the porch door wide and waited while she stepped in. The smell of roast chicken chased away any pale arguments she might have raised about staying for dinner. She used to grab quick food as she prepared orders at the café. She'd never worried about cooking or grocery shopping at home because she ate on the job. Now?

Truth to tell, she'd been barely eating at all. The realization smacked her upside the head as she crossed to Charlie's big recliner. "Hey, there. We had a great day today, thanks to Max's overnight efforts."

"Yeah?" Charlie's smile was a thin portrait of the one they knew so well. Tiredness dogged his eyes. "Max and Earl got all that stuff fixed?"

"We did. And how about we have you move into the living room, Dad, because when Beeze comes in from the lake, he's going to smell pretty bad. I'll leave him outside for a while, but then I'll tuck him on the porch. If that's all right."

"I can towel him off when he's done with his swim," Tina added. "Then he can curl up by the heater. He and I are used to this routine."

"Are you now?" Max lobbed an old towel her way from the stack they kept inside the back door. "You're elected, then. Need a hand, Dad?"

"I wouldn't mind one." Charlie huffed as he pressed his hands against the wide arms of the chair. He pushed down hard, but paused midway to catch his breath.

Max didn't fuss, he didn't act the least bit concerned or surprised, which told her he was skilled at pretense, and that wasn't something women put in the plus column. She'd had her share of guys who pretended to be happy. Never again. Still, his calm demeanor and strong arm beneath his father's elbow allowed Charlie the extra support he needed, and Max's matter-of-fact manner kept the moment drama-free. "Do you want to eat at the table or in the family room? There's an eight-o'clock game on ESPN."

"Who'd you say was playing?"

Tina sucked a breath. Charlie Campbell knew sports like no other. He loved catching games on TV, and he'd installed a TV in the hardware store so he could catch Pittsburgh throughout both seasons, baseball and football. He'd been celebrating their growing success all year. Before chemotherapy muddled his mind, Charlie would never forget what game was on, who'd scored the most points or who landed on the disabled list.

But he had.

He passed a hand across his forehead as he settled into the firm family-room chair. "They said I might forget stuff."

"It appears they were right," Max teased. "But Dad, that's normal for chemo. And it all comes back later."

Charlie stared at Max, stared right at him with a look that said too much, but then he shrugged, playing along. "That'll be good."

Tina's heart sank. For just a moment, she read the realization in Max's eyes, his face-off with the grim reality of a new timeline, but then he leaned in, hugged his father and backed off. "I'll bring you a tray, okay?"

Charlie's face paled further, and Tina hadn't thought that was possible. She touched Max's arm to draw his attention to "Plan B." "Or Charlie and I could just sit and talk while you guys eat," she offered brightly. "I'll fill him in on store stuff and pick his brain about the festival of lights."

"Since I want to be in on that conversation, I bet Mom won't mind if we hold off supper for a few minutes while we figure this out. Great idea, Tina."

His praise warmed her. His expression said he recognized her ploy and approved. It was clear that Charlie didn't want food, and despite the great smells emanating from Jenny Campbell's kitchen, Tina didn't mind waiting. Not if it helped Charlie.

Max set a side chair alongside Tina's in the family room and took a seat. She pulled a notebook and pen out of her purse. "Charlie, can you give us a quick overview of your normal festival timeline? Max has offered to help, but he hasn't been here since this tradition started."

Ouch. Salt in the wound... Max angled her a look she ignored.

"I've got some notes on my laptop. I'll have Mom get you the file," Charlie promised Max, but then added, "Thing is, I go my own way most times, and your mother told me I should write stuff down, but I was stubborn—"

A distinct cough from the kitchen said Jenny heard and agreed.

"So some of this I just roll with as it happens."

"Tell me those parts, Dad, then I can roll with it in your place."

Charlie explained the contracted light display in the park and the circle of lights surrounding the lake supplied by year-round home-owners and lakeshore businesses. A few cottage owners came back in December, too, solely to set up light displays at their summer homes. "The *Kirkwood Lady* takes dinner cruises around the lake after Thanksgiving," he added. "It only holds three dozen diners, so it gets booked up fast, but it's a sight to see, the boat, all lit up, circling the lake, surrounded by Christmas lights."

The image painted a pretty picture. The big boat, all decked out, surrounded by a ring of lights, trolling the lake's perimeter.

Max had been raised on the water. He'd learned how to fish, catch bait, water-ski and swim, all along the shores of Kirkwood Lake. But since the Sawyer family tragedy, and with the exception of army-related maneuvers, he'd purposely stayed on land. Losing his best friend, knowing what led up to that tragic night and how he might have prevented the heartbreak that followed, spoiled the beauty of lakeshore living.

As Tina jotted down information about the contracted lighting company, Charlie's eyes drifted shut.

"Supper's ready." Jenny walked into the room, saw Charlie and didn't hide the look of concern quite quick enough.

"We tuckered him out." Tina stood, leaned over, kissed Charlie's forehead, then moved toward the kitchen as if Charlie's slumber was the most natural thing in the world.

It wasn't, and Max felt funny leaving his father sleeping in the chair, worn from the influx of medications. He hesitated and remained seated. "I could just sit with him while he sleeps."

Jenny shifted her attention from son to husband and back, then she crossed the room, took Max's arm and drew him up. "He'd feel bad if you skipped eating, and the smell of food doesn't sit well with him now, so come to the kitchen, eat with us, and then you can sit with him. The doctors told us to expect this, all of this." The wave of her hand included Charlie's tiredness, his lack of appetite, aversion to smells and the loss of hair. "Though telling us didn't prepare me for the reality of watching him struggle." She hugged Max's arm as they moved into the kitchen he'd loved as a youth. "We'll take each day as it comes. I'm so glad you're here to help out, Max. I truly don't know what I would have done without you. Just having you at the store with Tina has taken such a load off his mind. Last night was the first peaceful night's sleep he's had since his diagnosis a few weeks ago. I can't tell you how happy that makes me."

Her affirmation confirmed two things for Max. First, he'd made the right decision in coming home. Second? He'd waited far too long, and if God allowed do-overs Max would be at the front of the line, begging. But for now he'd do what he could, when he could, making things easier for his parents. Yes, it meant he'd have to face the past—

And sooner or later he'd run into someone from the Sawyer family. Wanting to take charge of the situation, he decided to make the trip to the Sawyer house a priority. Knock on the door, walk in and talk to Pete's parents. Would they hate him for not stopping Pete from taking the boat that night?

Maybe. And they'd be justified in feeling that way. But owning his part in his friend's accident was the right move to make. And way overdue.

"That was amazing." Tina glanced at the messed-up dinner table and made a face. "I think I ate half that pan of chicken and biscuits. Which means you two didn't get enough, and while that should make me feel guilty, I'm too happy and full to apologize properly."

"Not eating right lately?"

Max's question made her squirm because she wasn't looking for sympathy or someone to watch over her. She'd just been downright hungry and Jenny was a great cook.

Downright hungry? I'd go with ravenous. Quick, there's one last biscuit. Don't let it get away!

"You don't know this, but we had a fire once, Tina, a long time ago." Jenny leaned forward, hands folded. "Charlie and I were newlyweds, living in an apartment in Clearwater. We were saving like crazy to buy a house of our own. Our oldest son, Marcus, was a baby and we'd broken the smoke alarm. I meant to buy a new one, but it was winter, Marcus had a bad cold and I didn't get out to the stores.

"A space heater in the apartment below us caught fire. Dad was working for the town, and he'd been called in to run the road plows. Marcus woke up to eat." She frowned, glanced down and clenched her hands tighter. "I wouldn't have known there was a fire if that baby hadn't been hungry. What if he hadn't woken up? Already the smoke was coming through the vents and the heat ducts. I grabbed Marcus and a big coat and some blankets for him, and we got outside, but for weeks afterward, all Dad and I could think was what if he hadn't woken up? There was no smoke detector, and we knew it. I could barely live with myself, Tina, imagining what-ifs. I couldn't eat and I don't think I slept for more than minutes at a time. It was crazy."

Tina had been doing exactly the same thing. Not eating, barely sleeping. But she'd spent so long pretending everything was okay in her world that having someone—even Jenny Campbell, mother extraordinaire—recognize her weaknesses seemed to put her at risk.

"For once Marcus's demanding personality did us some good." Max's joke eased the moment, but Jenny didn't let it go. She reached a hand over to Tina's and said, "Charlie and I will support whatever decisions you make, but we want you to know how much we love having you in Kirkwood. We'll do whatever it takes to help you reestablish your business if you decide to do that here. Now, I know you're thinking of starting over elsewhere, so I'm not saying this to pressure you," she added as she stood. "But we wanted you to know we're on your side, Tina."

Jenny's promise of help during this time of personal struggle should have made Tina feel good.

It didn't.

She didn't want to be torn. She didn't want to weigh options or decisions or pros and cons. She didn't want to talk to God about it, or waste more time than was absolutely necessary.

She just wanted to leave. Put it all behind her and go, brushing the dust of her family-less hometown off her feet like Jesus directed the disciples to do. She didn't want to think about broken engagements, loss of family and burned-out businesses. She wanted a clean slate, a new beginning.

Alone? You really want to start all over, someplace else? Absolutely alone?

Jenny's sincerity made Tina's decision to pull up stakes and leave town seem less inviting.

Beezer whined at the door. Jenny started to turn, but Tina raised her hand. "I promised Max I'd towel him off when he was ready to come in. I'll get him, Jenny."

"Thank you. I'm so distracted lately that I'm afraid I'll forget to take care of him while I'm helping Dad."

Tina grabbed her hoodie and went out the front porch door. She toweled Beezer off, then brought him into the warmth of the enclosed porch. "Here you go, old buddy." She switched the radiant heater on and laid one of Beeze's favorite worn blankets on the floor.

"You *have* done this before."

Approval softened the deep timbre of Max's tone. He stepped down onto the porch and reached low to pet Beezer. "He was little more than a pup when I joined the service."

"Yup."

"He's gotten old."

"That'll happen." She couldn't sugarcoat things for him. Sure, he was devoted to the service, to making rank, to moving up, but he'd stayed away on purpose. And that was inexcusable.

"I wish I'd been here."

His honest admission defused her resentment. She expected him to make excuses, to launch a well-prepared defensive explaining his choices and lauding his service.

He did no such thing. He just sank down onto the floor and petted the old dog's head silently.

She didn't know what to say, what to do. He'd surprised her. She'd spent years wishing she had a family like this, a family that clung together through thick and thin, while Max had brushed them off.

But she hadn't expected outright, blatant honesty. Hearing his regret said she might have been too harsh in her initial assessment.

"Do you have a dog, Tina?"

She'd never had any pets. Why was that? she wondered, seeing the love bond reignite between Max and Beeze. "I don't, no."

"But you're so good with him." Max tipped his head back and looked at her, and there it was again, that glimmer of assessment, appraisal. "Like you're born to love animals."

"I get my share of loving when I come over here," she told him. She stood, gathered her purse and slung it over her shoulder crosswise. "That's plenty. It's tough to give an animal all the love and care it needs when you're working all the time."

His nod said he understood.

His eyes said something different altogether.

But no matter what Max thought, Tina understood the motivations behind her singular actions. When everything you've ever loved…or thought you loved…went away, alone was just plain better.

Max's cell phone buzzed him awake in the middle of the night. He answered it quietly, not wanting to disturb his parents, but knowing it must be important for his brother Seth to place a call at that hour. "What's up? Do you need help? I can be there in five minutes."

"Only if you break all the speed limits, and yes, I need you here. Now."

Max was half-ready before his brother placed the request. "Are you okay? Is it the babies? What's going on?"

"My family's fine," Seth assured him.

Max breathed a sigh of relief. Seth's wife, Gianna, had given birth to fraternal twins in early summer. Mikey and Bella were the sweetest things God ever put on the planet, and he'd felt a fierce shot of protective love when he'd met them for the first time the week before.

"Someone was snooping around the remains of Tina's place on the water, then cut through the pass between the church and the hardware store. I'd just finished feeding Mikey and saw a flash of movement at the edge of the light. I don't think he or she knows they've been spotted."

"I'm on my way."

Max bolted for the car once he'd quietly closed the kitchen door to the side entrance. He started the engine, backed out of his parents' drive slowly, then picked up speed as he cruised toward the village at the northern point of Kirkwood Lake. In town, he drove past the hardware store as if it was perfectly normal for traffic to pass through Kirkwood in the middle of the night. He turned right onto Overlook Drive, passed Seth's house deliberately, then let the car glide to a silent stop. He turned the engine off, slipped from the driver's seat and leaned the door shut. If anyone was still around, he didn't want to ruin the false sense of security he'd just created.

His eyes adjusted to the darkness quickly. He spotted Seth's unmoving frame at the far edge of his carriage-style garage. Max walked around the garage, hoping Seth recognized his maneuver. When Seth melded back into the shadows on the far side of the angled garage, Max knew he understood. They met up on the farthest, darkest edge of the building. "Have you seen him again?"

Seth shook his head. "No. But I've been watching to see if he came back."

"Was he at the hardware store? Do you think someone's trying to break in? Or set another fire?"

Backlit by the outside house lights, Max couldn't see Seth's face, but he read the consternation in his tone. "I'm not sure. It seemed the original intent was to find something in the ashes of the café."

"This person was crawling through a roped-off crime scene?"

"Yes."

Max could only think of one reason why anyone would grope their way through the ashes of Tina's cafe in the middle of the night: to find something that might incriminate them. "Man? Woman? Child?"

"No way to tell. Too far and too dark. But whoever it was moved quick and light."

"Probably a woman or a kid."

"I hate to think either," Seth admitted, "but that was my gut reaction, too."

"I'll go the long way around the store, circling the outside of the church and the cemetery behind," Max said. He clicked his watch to mark time. "In four minutes you come around the front to the back entrance of Dad's store. I'll flash my pen from the edge of the cemetery woods. And we'll go in together."

"You packing?" Seth wondered aloud.

"Always." Skill with handguns had become intrinsic to Max years ago. Going through life armed and ready was second nature now.

"Just don't shoot me, okay?"

"It *is* dark," Max whispered as he slipped along the back of the garage, then into the shadows of the tree-lined street. Strewn leaves would have marked his presence on a dry night, but the late-day rain silenced his movement. He slipped along the front edge of the graveyard, then through the forested southern border. If this person was targeting area businesses to burn, or searching to remove incriminating evidence, Max was going to make sure he or she didn't get any farther than Dad's hardware store parking lot. Unless they'd already made their way home, wherever that was, and in that case, they'd let the authorities figure it out. Right now, with Seth covering his back, Max knew he was in the driver's seat.

"Stop right there."

Max froze.

"I've already called the police, and if you move, I'll—"

"Tina?" He turned, hands up, and peered into the trees. "Where are you?" he whispered. "What do you think you're doing?"

"Max?"

If there'd been time or if he was sure she wasn't pointing a gun at his back, he'd have banged his head against one of the nearby trees in frustration. As it was, he held perfectly still until he made out her shape—well, half her shape—behind one of the sprawling maples planted nearly eighty years before. For one split second he wondered if it had been Tina that Seth had spotted in the rubble...but it couldn't have been.

Could it?

Why would Tina be snooping around the ruins of her burned-out café, the place she loved so much?

She's pretty anxious to leave this town behind. Anxiety can push people to do things they'd never do normally.

"I saw someone," she whispered as she crept through the trees.

Tina lived in an upstairs apartment on Overlook Drive, kitty-corner from Seth's house. Her front windows overlooked Kirkwood Lake and Main Street. At this point, Max was actually surprised they hadn't been joined by a cast of thousands, which was just as likely as having four people roaming Main Street in Kirkwood in the dead of night. "What did you see?"

"Someone moving around the timbers of the café."

"And do you make it a habit of being up in the middle of the night, checking out Main Street?"

"I didn't used to," she retorted, and he didn't have to listen hard to hear the sting in her voice. "I used to sleep soundly. And then someone burned down my business, and I'm lucky I sleep at all. And at this point, the three hours I got tonight will probably be it, because how can I crawl back into bed and fall asleep after all this?"

Jenny's words rushed back, how she'd lost sleep and her appetite in the aftermath of an accidental fire as a young mother. How much worse must it be to think you were targeted?

Tina pointed west toward Seth's house. "I woke up and saw Seth's lights on. I worried that one of the babies might be sick. When he came creeping outside, I knew something was up. I looked further and saw something. Someone," she corrected herself, "moving through the remains of the café."

"Doesn't anyone sleep around here anymore?" Seth's voice entered the conversation from the near side of the church parking lot.

"It appears not." Max decided the time for subterfuge was over. He flicked the flashlight of his cell phone on. "Tina saw someone, too."

"She did, huh?" Seth moved forward, frowned, then yawned. "Well, between the three of us, we've managed to give away any tiny advantage we might have had. Max, did you see anything?"

"Other than Tina? No."

He directed the light toward her. She flushed.

"Me, neither. So whoever it was didn't hang around tonight, but I don't like that he or she hightailed it up here toward Dad's store when he thought he'd been spotted."

"Me, neither. I could start sleeping here. Add an ounce of Fort Bragg protection to the local mix."

"Mom would go crazy with that. And Dad would worry, and the last thing we want to do is make Dad worry."

"No argument there. So what do we do?"

"For now, go home." Tina offered the suggestion as she turned back toward Overlook Drive. "Although the likelihood of getting more sleep is pretty much impossible now."

"Because?" Max left the comment open-ended, hoping for the right answer. She supplied it, and wasted no time doing it.

"There's only one reason someone would be poking around the ashes of my hard work," she answered quickly, and he read the thick emotion in her voice. "And that's because they're looking for evidence that puts them at the scene of the fire. Which means the supposition of arson just became a reality in my head."

Chapter Four

She looked like someone had just stolen her best friend, her favorite toy and her puppy all at once. A sheen of tears brightened her eyes, and Max resisted the pull for sympathy until her chin quivered.

That did it.

He reached out and gathered her in for a hug. Tina's expression reflected the very emotions his mother had shared over supper. Fear. Questioning. Guilt. Remorse.

Not eating.

Not sleeping.

Barely existing.

He hugged her close, letting her cry against his shoulder. He heard Seth slip off into the shadows, retracing his steps back home. When the tears paused, he looped an arm around her shoulders and headed for the sidewalk.

"Where are we going?"

"I'm walking you home."

"This is the long way," she whispered, then scrubbed the arm of her sweatshirt across her face, total tomboy. "No tissues."

"I see that." He quirked a tiny smile down to her. "Could've asked me, you know."

"You carry tissues in your pocket?"

"No. But you could have asked."

Her smile said she was feeling better. She moved a step ahead and waved him off. "I can find my own way home. You don't have to walk me, Max."

He pulled her right back by his side and reestablished that arm around her shoulders. "I do. First, if there's someone lurking in the shadows, I can't exactly leave you alone to discover them, can I?"

"Well, no, I suppose not, but you don't need to put your arm around me."

"Wrong again. If anyone sees us, we want them to think we're taking a leisurely romantic stroll around town, not staking out felonious criminals."

"At four forty-five in the morning?"

"Last I knew there was no clock on romance, Tina. It is what it is."

"I actually prefer folks assuming we're on a clandestine mission than star-crossed lovers, Max. In this town, the latter gets you into a lot more trouble. Everyone knows and rarely forgets. Take it from the voice of experience." She paused and he did, too, looking down. "Fishbowl romance isn't fun."

"The joys of small-town living." He walked her past his car and to her door. "I'll see you at nine, okay? But if you do fall asleep and want to sleep in, that's fine. Earl's in early and we can handle things."

"I might, then. Thank you, Max."

She looked up at him. Met his gaze.

Maybe it was the flicker of fresh-washed moonlight now that the rain had passed. Maybe it was the way the soft night breeze lifted the short tendrils of her hair, dancing them around her face. Or the way her mouth parted slightly, looking up, as if wanting to say more...

Do more.

He breathed deep, holding her gaze, wondering what it would be like to lean closer. Touch his mouth to hers. See what Tina Martinelli was all about.

"Max, you want coffee?" Seth's rather loud attempt at whispering effectively ended the moment. "I figured it's late enough, we might as well start the day."

Tina stepped back.

So did Max.

And as Seth lumbered out of the shadows of his Dutch Colonial across the street, the sound of a car squealing east on Main Street said someone had just made a quick get-away, and in a tiny, quiet town like Kirkwood, the noise stood out. Blocked by trees and houses, they couldn't make out the car, or even ascertain where it had been parked, but that told Max two things: one, the car hadn't looked out of place, or Seth would have noticed it. Therefore the car was a regular visitor to this end of town.

And two, that they were on the right track in circling around the small business center of Main Street, Kirkwood Lake, because someone was up to no good.

The question was who?

He turned back toward Tina.

She'd paled at the sound of the car, and he didn't have to explain the car's presence or rapid retreat. The stark look of her face said she got it.

But wished she didn't.

"We'll figure this out," he promised. "In the meantime, you could always come stay at the house. Mom would love the company, and you wouldn't be alone."

Her jaw jutted, stubborn. "I've gotten used to being alone. And Seth's right there, across the street. Most people don't want to mess with a county sheriff if they can avoid it."

"But your apartment backs up to the cemetery and the woods leading to the highway," Max argued. "And Seth has to sleep now and again, although with two babies, that's a trick in itself." He didn't add that someone had torched the business not far from Seth's home, clearly not worried about a sleeping sheriff's deputy.

"I thank God for their grandmothers every day," Seth droned, yawning. "Shift work has proven to be a marvelous thing. But Max is right, Tina. Most arsonists target something. In this case it's either you—"

Max hated the stark look that came into her eyes as she glanced south toward the burned-out building.

"—Sol Rigby or the town. Sol's out on Log Cabin Road, and it's pretty tricky to get to his cabin without being seen. If it's the town, then this guy could strike again anytime. We took precautions on Gianna's business and the hardware store with increased security cameras and alarms, but that doesn't mean he can't get around those to start a fire. But what if he's targeting you personally, Tina?" Seth crossed his arms and stared her down, and instead of getting mad like she'd have done with Max, she looked resigned. "How do we keep you safe?"

"Right now, all I want is to be warm," she retorted. She pulled her hoodie tighter and moved toward the side door leading up to her apartment. "We'll discuss this later. Whoever it is has left for the night, and I can't think straight on little sleep and no coffee. Good night, guys."

She slipped into the side door, locked it, and Max and Seth waited until they saw her light blink on upstairs.

Max turned toward Seth. "I don't like this."

"Me, either."

"We're caught in the middle, not knowing what's really going on until we get to scene two, which is usually another fire."

"And no one wants that."

"But figuring this out with three diverse directions will take legwork."

"I'm calling the fire chief and the arson investigation squad once we're at first light," Seth assured him. "I don't know what this guy—"

"Or woman."

Seth acknowledged that with a nod. "What he or she was looking for, but the team will want to comb things carefully again before they can clean that mess up. Which means the eyesore of a burned-out building might be around for a while unless the investigators feel confident that they've got everything they need. Not exactly the draw for the Christmas light festival we hoped for. By the way." Seth pulled the storm door open and let Max move into the house ahead of him. "Do you need help with the festival stuff? I know everything's gotten kind of dumped on you, and it's your own stupid fault for staying away so long, but you are my kid brother and I'll help. If I have to."

Max started to laugh, realized the house was still mostly asleep, stifled the instinct and shook his head. "You take care of babies, that cute wife, your various new Italian relations and your job. Plus guarding the town. I can handle the lights."

His words sounded braver than he felt, but he'd put the lighting array folders into his car the night before so he wouldn't forget them this morning. If he grabbed some slow minutes at the hardware store today, he'd go through the schematics and get an idea of how the lake-wide show worked.

He'd tackled some pretty impressive jobs overseas. He'd learned to blend, build and dismantle secretive missions on a moment's notice. But those had been on the down-low. If he messed up no one but he and his team knew, and they were trained to improvise on a moment's notice.

Not one of those clandestine missions made him as nervous as the possibility of messing up Christmas for an entire town. If for no other reason than to make up for times he was a jerk as a teenager, Max wanted this festival to go right. It was the least he could do. And with the upcoming committee meeting, he'd be face-to-face with folks from his past, including Pete's mom. Truth to tell, he wasn't sure how to handle that.

"Max!" Mary Sawyer claimed a hug the moment she laid eyes on Max the next night. The embrace felt good... and bad all at once. The mix of emotions tunneled Max back in time. The Sawyers' beachfront yard, the campfire, the bottle Pete had paid a college guy to buy. If he'd put a stop to Pete's foolishness then, would Mary Sawyer's son and his girlfriend be alive now?

"It's so good to see you." Mary's warm voice softened his flashback. "Look at you! All grown up, and so handsome. We're so proud of you, Max." She gripped his arm in a show of support and affection. "I hope your mother's told you that. Every summer we put up honor flags along Main Street, remembering our men and women in the service, and I make sure yours is right there, dead center, for everyone to see. Welcome home, Max."

His heart churned.

Seeing Pete's mom, being wrapped in her motherly embrace, felt like old times. But Max was a trained army officer. He'd stayed alive doing clandestine work because he knew better than to wallow in false security. Mary Sawyer was gushing over him because she remembered the good times...

And because she didn't know the whole truth. Only

three people knew the full extent of what happened that hot August night, and two of them were gone.

Guilt climbed his spine, then tightened his neck. Several other committee members came through Carmen Bianchi's door just then, including Tina. One of them called Mary's name. She patted his cheek and moved off to talk with an unhappy-looking woman. Max didn't recognize her, but within two minutes of opening the meeting, he realized that if he was marking friend and foe, this woman would be firmly in the latter column.

"There's no way that can work," she insisted when Tina went through Charlie's basic plan. "You don't know me, Max Campbell, but I've been on this committee for eight years, and I can't believe we don't have a more detailed description of what goes where than that." She pointed to the folder of papers Max laid out on the table of Carmen's living room. "We have to have everything constructed and ready to go in a week. I don't see that happening."

"We've got a contract with Holiday Lighting out of Buffalo, Georgia." Mary Sawyer sent Georgia Palmeteer a calming look. "They take care of the park display. The town does the Main Street lighting, same as always, and Max will oversee the rest. Most folks do their own thing, so it's not like he even has all that much to do. I think he'll do just fine." She beamed a smile his way, and once again the thought of what should have been broadsided him. He needed to come clean, and he needed to do it soon because enduring her understandable wrath was far better than letting a nice woman like Mrs. Sawyer think he was a great guy.

Aren't you a great guy?

Now? Yes.

Back then? No.

Pete and Amy's accident was a long time ago. You were

a kid. Look at the facts, man. Your buddy had a wild streak those last couple of years. It wasn't your job to look after him.

Max knew better. They'd been friends a long time. Pete was like a brother to him, and if there was one thing Campbell brothers did well, it was take care of one another. When they weren't beating on each other, that is.

"We've left the majority of a massive fund-raiser in the hands of someone who doesn't write down what needs to be done," retorted Georgia. "That's plain carelessness."

"Oh, Georgia, really." Mary rolled her eyes. "It's gone fine every single year. Why are you all up in arms over this?"

"We Palmeteers like things done right," she snapped, and her pretentious tone said she didn't think all too much of Mary Sawyer's more casual attitude. "Leaving things to chance is for amateurs. Folks pay good money to come here for the drive through the park and the Main Street Festival. I, for one, don't take that lightly."

"Having Max on board offers us an opportunity for change," Tina remarked.

The committee shifted their attention to her.

"Max and the guys might not do everything exactly the way Charlie would have done it, but as long as we have everything lit and beautiful, what difference does it make?"

"Because we like things the way they are, young lady." Georgia's clipped tone said she didn't appreciate being brought to task by someone half her age.

"With an aging population, it's probably good for us to get used to change now and again," offered Carmen Bianchi as she rolled an old-fashioned tea cart into the room. "As the younger generation takes over, we have two options, to compromise and trust them to lead the way or give up. And I never give up on anything so, Max Campbell, you have my vote." She smiled at Max and indicated the cart with a dip of her chin. "I know this isn't as fancy as what we used to get at Tina's café, but Tina did the baking so we know that part is wonderful."

"Well, that's another thing," Georgia groused as she bustled to be first at the portable coffee setup. "Tina's done the majority of food for the park vendors and for our 'Christmas on Main Street' day. How are we going to manage this with her business gone? I say we tap into The Pelican's Nest restaurant and see if Laura will help with food. I mean, it seems silly not to ask her with Tina's place out for the count."

Georgia's careless words stabbed Tina's gut.

She'd half-expected someone to come up with this idea, and it wasn't a surprise that it was the town supervisor's ill-tempered sister, but to have her spout it here, in front of the whole committee, without putting it on the agenda or checking with her... She felt blindsided, and rightfully so. It wasn't as if the entire town didn't know her broken family history and the animosity Rocco had shown her for years.

Mary Sawyer turned toward Tina. "What do you think, Tina? County health laws say we need to produce food in a certified kitchen, so we can't just cook up a storm at home. Liability rules prevent that. How can we set this up?"

"We have a couple of options," Tina replied. She felt Max's gaze, but kept her attention focused on the other committee members as they helped themselves to coffee and cake. "Certainly we can ask Laura to help. We've done that in the past and, if you remember, Rocco made it clear he wasn't about to undercut his business by feeding folks in the street."

Several nods said they all remembered Rocco's mean-spirited replies.

"But with Rocco gone, Laura might be more willing to help. Who would like to ask her?"

No one spoke up, but then Carmen Bianchi raised a hand. "I will, dear. No harm in trying, I always say, and I don't know Laura so there's no hard feelings either way."

"Thank you, Carmen." Tina smiled at the aging Italian woman and quietly thanked God for bringing Carmen Bianchi and Gianna Costanza to town the year before. The two expert seamstresses had brought a thriving business and warm, open hearts to Main Street, a definite plus for the popular village.

"With or without Laura's help, we'll be fine," she went on, and when a couple of people raised skeptical brows, she met their unspoken concerns head-on. "I haven't been spending these four weeks with my head in the sand. Piper Harrison has offered the use of their kitchen at the McKinney Farms Dairy store. And Lacey Barrett has done the same at the apple farm across from the Campbell house on Lower Lake Road. If we set up the heated tent on Main Street like we always do, we can have food prepped at either or both of those locations, and we can do on-site cooking/grilling right in the food tent like we've done in the past."

"That would work just fine," Mary announced. "Tina, thank you for making those arrangements. And I know the fire department is excited to be manning the grill as always."

"Perfect." Tina smiled at her, glad that her legwork had defused the situation. "And—"

"Well, that's another thing," Georgia interrupted with a tart glance to Carmen's east-facing window. "How in the name of all that's good and holy are we going to have a pretty, sweet, inviting Christmas festival with the mess from Tina's fire just sitting there, getting wetter, soggier, smellier and sloppier every day?"

Tina's heart froze, the very heart that had built a thriving business over years of hard work and sweat equity. It didn't matter that she felt the same way. To have Georgia throw it up in her face in a sneering, I'm-better-than-everybody way cut deep.

"It may not be a problem."

Attention shifted to Max. He splayed his hands, clearly comfortable with taking charge as he stood and moved toward the group. "The investigation into the fire is still incomplete. I know the arson squad feels the need to comb through the remains of Tina's coffee shop to find clues about who would do this kind of thing, but I also know they've slated the comb-through for tomorrow. After that, we should be able to schedule the big equipment for demolition and removal."

"They can get it done that quickly?" Mary Sawyer looked impressed.

"The change in the weather is pushing them," Max told her. "And they know the town needs to put a sad piece of history behind them and move on."

"But what if he strikes again?" wondered Jason Radcliffe, another committee member. "I've been a volunteer fireman for years. Arson is rarely a single-crime event. How do we protect the town and the festival? I can't pretend I'm not concerned about that."

"Me, too."

Again all eyes turned to Max, and Tina had to give it to him. His squared-off, rugged but calm stance said he'd do whatever it took to get the job done. And when he smiled at Georgia Palmeteer, Tina was afraid the older woman might keel over on the spot. Clearly her sour temper didn't make her immune to Max's dark good looks and take-charge style.

"But that's why the squad wants to get this done. If there's evidence to be found at the scene, they might be able to make an arrest before the festival and that would put an end to our concerns."

"Oh, it would!" Georgia nodded as if Max was the smartest—*and cutest*—thing on the planet.

"It would be a relief," Carmen agreed. "The thought that someone could destroy another person's hopes and dreams is a shock in such a wonderful town."

Her words provided the balm to close the meeting peacefully. As Tina tugged her coat from the row of hooks inside Carmen's kitchen door, strong hands reached over hers, withdrew the coat and held it open for her to put on.

"Thank you, Max."

He frowned at the coat, then her. "It's too cold for this jacket."

"I only have to go up the hill to get home." She tugged her coat sleeves down over her hands to avoid the deepening chill. "And it wasn't this bad when I headed down here. I must have missed the weather report that said arctic air was nose-diving into Kirkwood Lake."

"Lows in the twenties," Max advised. He turned toward Carmen and gave her a big hug. "You did great. Thank you for hosting the meeting and for your vote of confidence. I wasn't sure which way things would go right then, but your words tipped the scales. I'm grateful."

"Well, it's much ado about nothing," Carmen replied. "When folks don't have big things to concern themselves with, they pay too much attention to little things."

Her words hit home with Max.

Self-satisfaction wasn't an easy lesson learned. He'd learned to like himself in the service, and had earned his share of respect and responsibility along the way, but he'd had a hard time wrapping his head around what he needed versus what he wanted.

He needed to be forgiven. That might or might not happen, but he couldn't be back in town and walk in the shadow of old lies and live with himself. Which meant he needed to set things straight with the Sawyers, a task he'd do as soon as time allowed.

On top of that?

He longed to belong somewhere. To be part of something calm and quiet. He'd done the gung-ho thing to the best of his ability, but seeing his father's decline and his mother's worry showed him a dark mirror image. He'd let shame keep him at bay for too long. His unexplained absence hurt his parents and his family. He would never do that to anyone again. "Thanks again, Carmen. I'm going to see Tina home—"

"Are not."

Max ignored her and continued, "Then I'm going to set up camp at the hardware store, but I'm going to leave my car stashed behind Seth's place."

"You're baiting a trap." Approval laced Carmen's comment. "Gianna told me what Seth and Tina saw last night." Carmen directed her gaze toward the window that faced Tina's burned-out shop. "It's creepy to think someone was out there, snooping around in the dead of night while I was sleeping. What do you think he was hunting for?"

Max shrugged. "I'm not sure. But once word gets around that the arson investigators are going to go through the site, the perp is likely to come back for whatever he lost."

"So you guys are going on watch patrol, hoping you've tempted him or her out?"

"That's why I mentioned the time limit at the meeting,"

Max admitted. "This way word gets around, folks will yak it up, and the arsonist might show up."

"Unless I was the arsonist and you just warned me off," Tina countered, looking straight at Max, and the look on her face said she was voicing her own personal concerns. "Maybe I wanted out of town so badly I torched my own business."

"Tina, that's ridiculous," Carmen spouted. "Anyone in their right mind—"

"I expect it's what a few people might be thinking," Tina continued. "And I know the arson team investigated me."

Max put a hand to Tina's face, her cheek. He left it there, trained his gaze on hers and uttered one short sentence. "You didn't do it."

Her chin quivered.

She firmed it and pulled back, but the coat hooks got in her way.

"They have to investigate everyone, Tina," he continued. His low, level voice helped calm her frayed nerve endings. "That's the job of the arson squad. But we all know you would never do such a thing, so you need to relax. Shove off the urge to take offense, let the investigators do their job and keep helping me at the hardware store so I don't mess up Dad's business. And maybe we'll catch whoever it was you and Seth saw last night."

"You believe me."

Max's wry expression said that was about the stupidest thing he'd ever heard. "Woman, I never doubted it for a minute. No real coffee lover destroys a crazy-expensive espresso machine. It just isn't done."

He meant it.

He meant every single word even though people used insurance fraud to pad their budgets far too often. "I do love my coffee," she admitted. And then she smiled up at him, and he smiled down at her, and for just a moment there was no Carmen, there was no divisive meeting, there were no worries, there was just Max's smile, warm and soothing, the kind of smile a girl could lose herself in for oh…say…forever?

A rush of cold air changed the course of her thoughts as Max pulled Carmen's door open. They hurried through, closed the door, then headed up the sloped incline of Overlook Drive toward Tina's apartment.

Cold, biting wind didn't allow casual conversation, and when a strong gust tunneled down Overlook, Max grabbed hold of Tina's arm, gaining leverage for both of them.

And then he didn't let go.

Her heart did one of those weird flippy things girls talk about all the time, like it used to when she watched Max from afar fifteen years before.

Stop it, heart. Stop it right now!

Her pulse refused to listen. The grip of his hand on her arm, the solidity of him, the intrinsic soldier effect, combined to make her heart jump into a full-fledged tarantella.

Working side by side with him taught her something new. Max had changed in his time away. He was still crazy attractive, the kind of dream date any girl would want, but he was more now. He'd grown up to be a man of honor and strong character. Suddenly the two past relationships she had thought might end in happily-ever-after paled beside the valor of the U.S. soldier escorting her home. Did that make her fickle? Or stupid?

I'd go with smart, her conscience advised.

Tina wasn't so sure about that. She'd almost married one guy and had thought about it again with the other. So…not smart.

Wrong. The mental scolding came through loud and

clear as they approached Tina's door. *Why is it okay to notice Max has grown up and not realize you've done the same thing? Every princess kisses a toad or two. That's how we find Mr. Right. Eventually. And let me take you back to Sherrie's bit of advice... Have you given this to God? Prayed about it?*

She'd done no such thing, and the realization shamed her.

"We're here, we didn't blow away. And wear a warmer coat tomorrow. Please." Max added the last word when she frowned up at him, and the look he gave her, now that they were in the sheltered alcove of her door, said he wasn't just being bossy. He was concerned.

Her heart didn't flip this time.

It softened under his warm look of entreaty, as if her comfort mattered. From somewhere deep inside, an old feeling dredged up, a fledgling feeling of something good and warm and holy.

His gaze flitted to her mouth, then back to her eyes, wondering.

She stepped back into the doorway.

She'd put her heart on the line twice before. And even though it was no longer baseball season, every American understood the "three strikes and you're out" rule. Right now—

She paused, gazing up at Max, and realized she wasn't sure what she wanted right now, because when Max Campbell was around?

Her thoughts muddled.

"You did mention that you weren't seeing anyone." Max smiled down at her and touched one chilled finger to her cheek.

"And I have no intention of seeing anyone." She held his gaze, refusing to back down or step forward. "My short timeline says we need to leave things uncomplicated. We're coworkers." She squared her shoulders and raised her chin. "And that's only until I move away. I can't afford to get involved, I have a serious disregard for broken hearts and I'll be gone soon. The hardware store is slower in winter. That will give you time to train someone else to step in."

"They won't be as pretty," Max observed, but he took a step back.

And the minute he did? She wished he hadn't.

He glanced up. "Head in, get warm. I'll watch until your lights come on, then I'm circling around as if I'm leaving. That way if anyone's watching, they'll have the false assurance that I'm gone and Seth's on duty in Clearwater."

"Is he?"

"No. He's staked out inside the vestibule of the church. Reverend Smith was more than happy to give him a warm place for his watch."

"The reverend and his wife are good people." She thought the world of the Smiths, a wonderful couple. They seemed so strong, solid and peaceful in their faith. Sometimes she sat in the back of church, feeling like an imposter. Did she believe in God?

Yes.

Did she trust Him to take charge of her life, lead the way?

No.

Isn't that why He gave her two arms, two legs and a working brain? So she could run her life her own way?

How's that been working out for you lately? You might want to rethink that whole trust-in-God thing. Just a suggestion. She silenced the internal rebuke, but hadn't Sherrie been telling her that same thing lately? To put God in charge, play Him on the front line and not leave Him on the bench?

The very thought required courage she didn't have. "Be careful tonight."

"Will do. And remind me to order some kind of coffee service for the hardware store. It's crazy not to have a coffeemaker there."

Tina read what Max didn't say, that he felt funny patronizing her aunt's business when things were bad between them. She nodded, then paused. "I'll bring over my one-cup system. You buy the pods. But in the meantime, I'm okay with grabbing coffee from Aunt Laura's place. I think she could use the business and I'm pretty tired of having bad feelings surrounding me. Know what I mean?"

Max mentally counted her request as superachievement number one.

He knew exactly what she meant. He read it in her eyes. Old regrets wore on the soul, never a good thing. "I'll do that. Good night, Tina."

"Good night, Max."

He crossed to Seth's place once Tina's lights blinked on, then took his car for a short spin. He returned the back way, slid into a parking spot behind Seth's garage and wound his way through the trees to below the hardware store. From the shelter of an alcove he could watch the ruins of Tina's store.

His brother Luke, another deputy sheriff who lived farther down the east side of Kirkwood Lake, would take over the watch in two hours, allowing Max time to sleep. And Zach Harrison, a New York State Trooper who lived next to the McKinney Farm on the upper west side of Kirkwood Lake, had agreed to relieve Seth. They'd set up a schedule between them, knowing manpower was tight on their combined forces, but also aware of an arsonist's typical time frame. The emotional "high" of a fire wore off quick, and most arson-lovers struck again fairly soon. Seth, Luke, Zach and Max had decided among themselves that it wasn't going to happen on their watch.

And that was the beauty of a small town like Kirkwood, especially one front-loaded with a good share of first responders. The arsonist had used the element of surprise to his advantage when they'd torched Tina's café.

They refused to allow him or her to have that advantage again.

Chapter Five

Tina lugged the coffeemaker into the hardware store early the next morning. She assumed she'd lie awake half the night, thinking about fire and arson and being alone.

She didn't. For the first time in weeks she fell into a sound sleep quickly and slept through the night. Why?

Because Max was watching over things.

When he's here, her conscience chided.

The sage advice hit home. Life taught her to tread carefully now. She had no desire for another broken heart or to be the object of conversation in their small town. She'd been there, done that.

It wasn't a bit fun.

First, falling for Max would be a game changer and she was done with games.

Second, she knew his style. When the going got tough? Max did his own thing. She'd seen that with the Sawyers, then with his family. And how anyone could take a wonderful family like the Campbells for granted...

Reason enough to run scared right there.

She was leaving, anyway. And even if she wasn't ready to wipe the dust of her hometown off her heels, it would take more than Max's word to convince her he was back in Kirkwood to stay. He'd traveled the world, gone on secret missions, played G.I. Joe to the max. The likelihood of Max setting up house in their quaint, sleepy, lakeside hometown?

Thin. And Tina was done with thin promises and broken dreams. She set up the coffeemaker, filled the water dispenser, then hesitated, caught between her bravado from the previous night and the cold light of morning.

She'd told Max that she wanted to mend things with her aunt. Had she meant it?

Yes. But could she do it?

She sighed, made a face and walked to the front window. To the right lay the church, white wood and stone, a sweet country remembrance of putting God first, a lesson she needed to embrace more often.

To the left and slightly uphill was The Pelican's Nest, the lakeshore eatery her parents had owned for decades. She'd taken her first steps there. She'd learned how to read there. She'd had her first kiss there, on the back steps of the kitchen, when Brady Davis dared her to kiss him.

Afterward, she couldn't for the life of her figure out what all the fuss was about. A few years later, watching Max Campbell date girl after girl, she got a clue. It wasn't the kiss—in fact it had very little to do with the kiss. It was the person you were kissing that made all the difference.

She glanced at the clock, saw she had plenty of time, then walked out the door and across the street to the restaurant entrance.

It felt odd walking through the front door. She'd always breezed in and out of the kitchen entrance, laughing, talking, working, her days and nights filled with school and The Pelican's Nest.

She hauled in a deep breath, pulled open the door and strode in.

Two customers she didn't know glanced up from the counter, nodded and went back to their coffee. Just two customers in the whole place, at prime breakfast time on a weekday morning.

"Can I help you?" Laura turned, saw Tina and stopped.

Tina took advantage of the surprise and moved forward as if everything was all right. "Can I have three coffees to go, Aunt Laura?"

"Of course." Laura half stammered the words. A pinched look said she wasn't sure what to say or what to do so Tina helped once again.

"I need room for cream and sugar in two of them. And if you have fresh Danish or coffee cake on hand, that would be nice, too."

"Three of them?"

"Sure. Any mix will do. We'll share."

An awkward silence ensued while Laura put the order together. There was no typical morning smell of sizzling bacon or rich French toast grilling alongside eggs over easy. Tina recognized the coffee cake as a recipe her mother had perfected two decades ago, a buttery-rich cinnamon concoction with melt-in-your-mouth texture. Tina's love of pastry making came from her mother, her love of restaurants from her father, and her stubborn nature had been a combo package. As Laura wrapped the square hunks of cake, she thought of the family they'd been so long ago.

Where had that gone? Why had it ended?

Illness, then greed. Her father's weakening condition pushed him to sell. Rocco's greed put her out on the street. But Aunt Laura...

"I'm sorry, Tina." Laura paused from the simple task. She bit her lip, then squared her shoulders and looked up.

Met Tina's gaze. "So sorry. Losing your coffee shop like that, after all the work you did."

Tina stood silent, unsure what to say. There was so much more to be sorry for, their histories intertwined, then butting heads.

"No matter what went on before, it broke my heart to see it happen."

Sincerity laced her words. For the first time in a lot of years, Tina felt the grace of sympathetic family, and it pricked emotions she'd thought long-buried. "Mine, too. Thanks, Aunt Laura."

Laura nestled the drinks into a tray, bagged the wrapped cake squares, added plastic forks and napkins and set the bag alongside the drinks. For just a moment she faltered, as if not sure how to charge Tina, but Tina pulled a twenty from her pocket and handed it over without waiting for a total.

Laura drew a breath, hit the register keys, then handed Tina's change back.

Tina wanted to tip her, tell her to keep the change, but she understood the restaurant business like few others. First, you never tip the owner. It just wasn't done.

Second?

Laura would be insulted. Tina knew her well enough to understand the awkward dynamics between support and charity. Support wasn't a bad thing.

Charity?

Martinelli pride would fight that, tooth and nail.

She lifted the bag in one hand and the drink tray in the other. "Thank you." She turned to go, but Laura called her name softly. She turned back. "Yes?"

"You were busy over there."

Tina didn't deny it. "Yes."

"I could use some of that here." Laura glanced around

the diner, and her expression said the lack of business was customary. Tina was restaurant-savvy enough to hear a death knell when it rang in front of her. Aunt Laura was going to lose The Pelican's Nest.

"Well, your competition's pretty much gone," Tina remarked. "Maybe things will pick up."

Laura frowned, and Tina had the strongest urge to hug the older woman.

She resisted.

"I want business to pick up, but not at your expense, Tina."

Not at Tina's expense?

Laura's words dredged up raw feelings.

She hadn't worried about Tina's expense when she turned her out on the street, no job, no family and no college education shoring her up. She hadn't worried when Tina worked night and day a block away, building a cozy, inviting enterprise, the kind of place The Pelican's Nest used to be, in the shadow of her aunt and uncle's business.

She and Rocco had taken Tina to court, tying up time and a legal defense that took years to pay off at fifty dollars a month, saying she violated the non-competition clause of the sale agreement. Even though they were planning to move south, her parents had agreed not to open another restaurant within eight miles of The Pelican's Nest for at least ten years, a common practice in the sale of a family business.

The judge threw the case out, but not until Tina had wasted time and finances fighting the pointless suit. As the judge pointed out, Laura and Rocco had made the agreement with Tina's parents.

Not with Tina.

And that was that.

But they had to know that fighting a court proceeding

was a huge setback for a young person trying to set up their own business. Which is exactly why they'd done it. But now, with Rocco gone, maybe Laura saw things differently. Tina hoped and prayed it was so. "I'd like them to find whoever set that fire and lock them away for a good, long time. Although maybe the fire was my cue to go elsewhere. Start over." She lifted the tray and the bag of baked goods. "To everything there is a season…" She left the quote open-ended deliberately. It had always been one of her father's favorites, and Laura was his younger sister.

"And a time to every purpose under the heaven." Laura finished the popular Ecclesiastes saying and nodded. "It's a lesson I should have learned a long time ago."

"Maybe now's the time." Tina moved to the door and smiled when one of the customers got up and opened it for her. "Thanks."

"Don't mention it, miss."

She started through the door, then stopped. Turned back. "Aunt Laura?"

"Yes?"

Tina's heart stammered in her chest. Old emotions fought for a place, but she shoved the negative feelings back where they belonged. "I could use your help."

"Help?"

Tina would have to be blind to miss the uncertainty and surprise in her aunt's eyes. She stepped back in and nodded. "The festival. I always did the baking for the vendor booths, but I've got no ovens now. Piper and Lacey both offered their baking areas, but they're not close enough for me to manage the baking and the running to keep fresh supplies going. Do you think I could do it here? In the restaurant kitchen?"

Her aunt's face brightened, but then she hesitated, looking embarrassed. "I don't have supplies, Tina. Or money for them."

"That's all covered under my budget," Tina assured her. "All I need is baking space. And I know your ovens aren't geared for major baking, but they'd work fine in a pinch. If you don't mind."

She'd extended an olive branch. Would her aunt take it?

Laura glanced toward the kitchen, then back to Tina. "I think it's a great idea, Tina."

Tina released a breath she didn't know she was holding. "Me, too. I'll have to come over here early."

"Can I help?"

"Sure, I'll—"

"I missed the bus again."

A young voice interrupted the moment. Tina turned and spotted Ryan, her fourteen-year-old cousin. He didn't notice her at first. His gaze was trained on his mother, his expression sullen and defensive. A bad combo.

"I got you up." Laura stared hard at the boy, then the clock. "You were in the shower when I left."

"I fell back asleep. So sue me."

Hairs rose along the back of Tina's neck. The boy's profile, the gruff tone, all reminded her of Rocco, and that tweaked a host of bad memories.

But then he turned more fully.

Ryan didn't look anything like Rocco from the front. Seeing him up close for the first time in a few years, he was the spitting image of her father, Gino Martinelli, in his younger days. Realizing that, she pushed aside her assumptions and said, "Ryan, you need a ride? I'll run you over to school."

He turned, surprised, then paled when he recognized her.

"Tina, could you?" Laura turned, her voice appreciative.

"No." Ryan's quick refusal drew the interest of one of the guys sitting at the counter.

"Well, you have to get to school and I can't take you," Laura reminded him. "In case you haven't noticed, I have a business to run."

Ryan glanced around, as if searching for a third option.

"I'll run him over, Laura." The older man at the counter stood, stretched and yawned. "I've got to go home and catch some shut-eye before the next shift, and it's on my way. Come on, Ryan, let's get you an education so you don't end up working two jobs to make ends meet like I do."

"Thanks, Bert."

The older guy shrugged and waved. Ryan followed him out the door, but he turned and looked at Tina again before he left, like he couldn't believe she was standing in his mother's restaurant, talking.

He'd been a preschooler when she got tossed, and Rocco made sure that lines were drawn in the sand, with Tina on one side and the D'Allesandros on the other. She'd just blurred that line by coming over, asking for help, and maybe with a little more time they could erase the line altogether.

She'd like that.

Max strode into the hardware store just before nine. He'd left the house early to fulfill his end of the bargain. He'd driven to Clearwater, the small city tucked at the southern tip of Kirkwood Lake, stopped by the Walmart there and grabbed four boxes of varied one-cup coffee pods. Turning the corner into the back room, he saw that Tina had remembered to cart her brewer down to the store.

His coffee-loving heart leaped in approval.

And when he noted the steaming hot coffee and cake

from her aunt's restaurant, he wanted to hug her. Draw her close and tell her he was proud of her. But if he did that with two customers and Earl in the store, he'd create a groundswell of small-town conversation neither one wanted or needed.

He grabbed the third coffee, took a sip, moved out front and smiled his thanks to her over the brim. "Perfect, Tina."

Her expression said she understood he was praising her for more than the coffee, and the slight flush of her cheeks said he'd scored points in the good guy column.

Good.

He'd decided last night that he enjoyed gaining points with Tina Martinelli, and if he stopped to examine it, he might wonder why. But when she handed him a wrapped piece of tender apple cake, it became obviously clear.

Fresh.

Funny.

Beautiful.

Cryptic but kind, and she loved little kids, small animals and his family.

His heart opened wider, and he'd have loved time to explore these feelings, but the day flew by with little time to chat or flirt, and he was on watch duty again that night, so by the time they closed up shop, he needed to have his car disappear as if he'd gone home—

And then slip back into town like he'd done the night before.

"Are you guys working the same game plan tonight?" Tina asked softly as he turned the key in the back door lock.

"We are."

"Do you want supper first?"

"You asking me out, Tina?" He turned, grinning, and

her rise of color said she wasn't—and yet, she was. "What have you got in mind?"

"I did a stew thing in the slow-cooker, and there's plenty. But you probably want to get home and see your dad."

"Mom just texted that he's sleeping and she's going over to Luke's to help Rainey make some new kind of tres leches cake thing. So I'm free."

"Rainey's tres leches cakes are the best things on the planet," Tina said.

"I don't know," Max mused. "I heard something from my brother Seth about a sweet potato pecan pie that's won the hearts of the entire lakeshore. And that's saying something because that's a fair piece of geography, Tina."

"I'll have to remember to thank Seth for the kind words."

"Don't be too nice to him. It'll go to his head. Now." He stopped and braced one hand on either side of the door, effectively trapping her between him and the hardware store entry. "You're really inviting me to dinner?"

"Crock-Pot stew isn't fancy enough to be called dinner."

"Supper, then."

"Supper works."

"Then let's do this." He motioned to her car. "I'll bring my car up and after we eat I'll noticeably leave your place. Then I'll circle around back again."

Tina nodded, moved toward the steps, then paused. "Thank you for doing this, Max. The whole stakeout thing. I know it's not your fight—"

"My parents love you to pieces, so it is my fight," he corrected her. "You might be family by attrition and I'm Campbell by adoption, but if there's one thing about us Campbells, we take care of our own. I'll meet you at your place."

He parked on the street in front of Tina's apartment,

leaving the car in plain sight. When he followed her up the stairs to her apartment, he was pleasantly surprised. "Retro chic. I'm kind of surprised and intrigued. Where's June Cleaver hiding?"

Tina laughed and brought two plates over to the small enamel-clad table. "Necessity. I had no money, and the antique and cooperative shops had lots of this fun retro stuff really cheap, so I decided I'd go with it."

"These old bowls." Max lifted one of the pale blue Pyrex bowls into the air. "Grandma Campbell had these. And these cabinets look like the ones in Aunt Maude's old place over in Jamison."

"Cute, right?" His appreciation deepened Tina's smile. "I figured if I had to live in an apartment, I wanted it as fun and homey as I could get it."

"You've achieved your goal. Can I help with anything?"

"You're doing enough standing guard into the dark of night. Sit and eat."

Max didn't have to be asked twice. "You made bread?"

"Nope, bought it when I ran out at lunchtime. Rainey's got a nice baked-goods section over at the McKinney Farms Dairy store, and it's only five minutes away. I figured it would go well with stew."

"Beyond wonderful."

She turned.

Her chin tilted up. She met his gaze, and he knew the second the compliment registered, that the words were meant for her, not the bread, because her eyes brightened and she looked embarrassed.

"But—" he sat down, reached over and sliced a couple of thick hunks off the loaf of freshly warmed bread "—you warned me off, so I'm trying to keep my compliments to myself, to stay calm, cool and slightly detached. How'd I do today?" He asked the question as if wondering how his job performance was going, quick and casual.

"You got an A on detachment and a B- on cool." She sat in the chair opposite him and offered the grades as if the assessment was the least personal thing ever.

"A B-?" Max shook his head. "On my worst day I couldn't get a B-. No way, no how."

"Are you protesting your grade?" She set the ladle down, then looked surprised and pleased when he reached across the small table and took her hand in his for grace.

He gave her fingers a gentle squeeze. "Naw, no protest. The bad grade just gives me incentive to try harder. Be cooler. Although I'm not sure that's even attainable."

She laughed.

It felt good to see it, good to watch her relax. Smile. Joke around. From what he'd gleaned in his short time home, Tina hadn't had a lot to laugh about these past few years, and that was wrong by any standard. He held her hand lightly and offered a simple prayer, a soldier's grace, and when he was done, he held her hand just long enough to make her work to extract it.

She scolded him with a look that made him grin, and then they shared a hot, delicious meal in a walk-up apartment decked out in second-hand 1950s motif, and he loved every minute of it.

He wanted to linger but the clock forced him to leave.

She walked him to the door, then stayed back a few feet, creating distance. But Max hadn't served in the army for over a decade without achieving some off-the-battlefield skills.

He noted the distance with his gaze, then drew his eyes up. Met hers. "Nice ploy, but if I wanted to kiss you, I'd cross that three feet of space and just do it, Tina."

"Which either means you don't want to, or you're being

a gentleman and respecting my request to keep our lives uncomplicated." She sent him a pert smile. "Excellent."

"Except—" he opened the door to the stairway, then turned, smiling "—Uncle Sam trained me well. I *like* things complicated. Creates a challenge. But tonight?" He pulled a dark knit hat onto his head, and matching leather gloves from the pockets of his black leather jacket. "Duty calls."

He started down the stairs, mentally counting them as he went. If she called his name before step number ten, he'd won a major battle.

If she stayed silent?

Well, that meant there was more work to be done than he'd thought. He stepped down quickly, leaving it up to God and Tina. *One, two, three, four...*

Total silence followed him from above.

Five, six, seven, eight...

"Max?"

He stopped, turned and had to keep from power-fisting the air. "Yes?"

"Thank you." Her gaze scanned his cold-weather gear and the village beyond the first-floor entry window. "Like I mentioned before, this means a lot to me."

"You're welcome." He didn't wink, tease or do anything else. There was no need to. By calling his name, interrupting his departure, she'd shown her mix of feelings. She liked him and wished she didn't.

Would she hate him when she found out the truth about Pete and Amy? Their deaths affected her best friend, their family, the entire neighborhood, the town. And he had *known* Pete and Amy had been drinking and hadn't stopped them from going out.

Maybe the better question was this: Why wouldn't she hate him?

He glanced up as he swung open the driver's-side door. She waved from the window, and the sight of her, back-lit and centered in the white-framed pane, made his heart yearn for that kind of send-off on a regular basis.

Blessed be the peacemakers, for they shall be called children of God. That's what he wanted now. To be a different kind of peacemaker here at home. Twinkle lights blinked on throughout the town. By next week, everything would be fully decorated. They'd open the Festival of Lights with a prayerful ceremony on the church green, and then they'd "throw" the switch, lighting up the lake, the town, the park.

Right now, with the sweetness of the newly erected church manger and the decorated, lighted businesses flanking Main Street, a sweet surge of the blessed holiday engulfed him. Yes, they were lit up a little early with Thanksgiving still days off, but as he tucked his car away and slipped through the cemetery paths to take up his watch station, the sweet lights celebrating Christ's birth welcomed him home.

Chapter Six

Whoever had been combing the ashes of the café had either found what they were looking for or smelled a trap. Either way, nothing came of the men's combined maneuvers.

Jason and Cory Radcliffe stopped into the hardware store at closing time. "Tina, can we talk to you out back before you head out?"

"Sure." She led the firemen into the back room, then turned. "Bad news?"

Jason shrugged. "Well, not good news. We've done what we can, the arson squad has gathered their evidence, they know an accelerant was used, but there's no real indication of who did this and the site's dangerous. We've ordered the excavation equipment. They're going to clean the site tomorrow."

Clean the site.

It sounded so simple. Matter-of-fact. A decade of work, hopes and dreams purposely destroyed, then scooped away.

Her heart ached, but it was the right thing to do. She knew that. Still.

She didn't want to be on hand to see it happen, but that couldn't be helped. "I appreciate you letting me know, guys. Thank you."

They didn't look the least bit comfortable accepting her thanks, and when they were gone, Max cornered her at the register. "Cleanup time?"

"You were listening?" Her tone scolded. Her look followed suit.

He pointed a finger at himself and made a face that said of course he was. "Covert operator. That's what I do, Tina."

A tiny smile escaped as she accepted his pronouncement. "That doesn't exactly rank you higher on the trustworthy scale. Snooping is unattractive."

"Snooping's for amateurs. I was on an information-gathering mission. Highly professional. And I needed to be close by in case they made you cry."

"They didn't."

He smiled. "I know. Because I was right outside the door."

A tiny part of her heart stretched, thinking of Max watching out for her again. "Then you know they're excavating tomorrow."

"An empty lot can be considered a fresh palette."

It could.

And yet the thought of big equipment sweeping up the remnants of her life in Kirkwood bit deep. "It's got to be done," she admitted. "I just hate the thought of being around to watch it happen."

"Then we'll find something else to do," Max said as he locked the door "The weather's supposed to be fairly nice tomorrow, according to my mother. But for now, come with me."

Max crooked a thumb toward his Mustang. Tina grabbed her purse and warm jacket, then followed him to the door. "Come with you where?"

He pointed to the passenger seat. "You did supper last night. My turn."

"Max, I—"

"Don't disappoint my mother. She's been simmering red sauce and meatballs and made me promise to bring you. You can't insult a woman who spent half the afternoon cooking, can you?"

"You don't play fair."

His smile agreed as he backed the car around. "All's fair in love and war."

"Well, as long as we're at war. Okay, then."

He laughed, but as they pulled out of the hardware store parking lot, two big rigs rounded the corner of Main Street. A huge loader with a bucket and a large dump truck chugged down the road, then parked along the edge of her burned-out café.

The sight of them reignited Tina's internal reasons for leaving. Enough was enough.

But then Max hit the car radio. Christmas lyrics filled the air, the perfect accent to the growing number of decorated houses leading out of the village. The bright sight of her old, familiar town filled her with nostalgia.

She thought she wanted new, fresh and bright. But how much would she miss the familiarity of her hometown once she made the move?

Her phone vibrated an incoming text from Sherrie. I know U R busy but could use help with nursery. Ideas?

She had tons of ideas. Ones she'd imagined for herself as she watched her biological clock tick for years. The thought of happily-ever-afters and cute kids had filled her with anticipation. In her quest for the American dream of marriage and two-point-four kids, had she hurried things? Charging ahead and regretting at leisure had always been part of her profile. Had she done that in matters of the heart?

Maybe. But she needed to think more on that tomorrow. With Christmas music playing, and Max easing the smooth ride around lakeshore curves, she focused on answering Sherrie.

Tons, she texted back. Call me later, we'll make a plan.

Thank you! Sherrie's return text was immediate, which meant she was waiting, hoping Tina would help. Was Sherrie feeling pushed to hurry because Tina was leaving? They'd been best friends, always together, for over two decades. The idea of being too busy or too far away to be a true help to Sherrie seemed wrong.

"Max! Tina! Perfect timing!" Jenny's voice caroled a welcome as Max tugged open the side door a few minutes later. "Dad was just saying he could use some company."

Beeze padded their way, tail wagging, as if wondering how they got through the day at work without him. He pushed his big, golden head beneath Tina's arm, knowing she'd give him a thorough welcome.

"I'm going to wash up and get rid of the remnants of changing oil and replacing hoses," Max announced. He reached down to pet Beeze. Tina looked up. Met his gaze. And when he smiled as if seeing her with the dog, in his mother's kitchen, made him happy, her heart tipped into overdrive again. "Back in a few minutes."

"Okay."

She helped Jenny finish things up while Charlie sat nearby, talking over the events of the day, and by the time Max returned, supper was on the table and Beeze had been relegated to the front porch.

"I'm not all that hungry, but I'll sit with you." Charlie pulled out the chair where he usually sat. "As long as none of you pester me about eating."

"The smells aren't bothering you?" Tina asked.

"Not as much, no."

"Good." Tina beamed at him, happy to see him looking more at ease.

Jenny's sigh said she'd follow his direction about not fussing, but wasn't thrilled with his pronouncement, and Max just grinned and said, "More for me, Dad. Leftovers tomorrow. I'm okay with that."

"Earl will be thrilled, too." Tina held a forkful of pasta aloft and breathed deep. "I could live on pasta. Cooked any way, anytime. Short women should not have this kind of affinity for carbs. And the oven-roasted broccoli is perfection, Jenny. Thank you."

"I grabbed the broccoli right across the street at Barrett's Orchards," Jenny told her. "I love having all their fresh produce so handy."

"Lacey's apple fritters aren't anything to wave off casually, either," Max noted. "We did some racing through those orchards when we were kids," he added. "It was a great place to grow up. The farm on one side of the house, the lake on the other."

"Isn't it funny to have people live in the same area, but have such different experiences?" Tina observed as she twirled more spaghetti onto her fork.

"As in?"

She indicated the village north of them with a wave. "Living in town had its upsides, and I helped at the restaurant a lot, but there were no games of hide-and-seek in the orchard, or grabbing a boat and taking off to fish when they were biting. Not until I bought my own, anyway."

"You like to fish?" Max looked surprised when Tina nodded.

"Love it. That's how I kept my sanity running the café all these years. Some days I'd just grab my little rowboat with its pricey trolling motor and cruise the docks, looking for bass and perch."

"I haven't had fried jack perch in over a year," Charlie lamented.

"It's late for perch, isn't it?" Max glanced from the calendar to Charlie and Tina.

"You can find them here or there if the weather's good and the wind is from the south-southwest," Charlie said.

"Do you want to go out, Dad?" Max stopped eating and faced his father. "They're calling for a nice day tomorrow. Sunny. Wind out of the south. I can grab a few hours off and take you around the lake. We could catch enough for a family fish fry between us."

"I'll go out with you when I'm feeling better," Charlie replied. "But the thought of eating fresh perch sounds mighty good. As long as you boys don't mind cooking it in the garage. The smell might be a little tough, otherwise."

"That's what the old stove is for," Max declared. He looked at Tina.

Something in his expression said he'd do this, but could use help. Which was just plain silly because a guy like Max didn't need help with anything. With tomorrow's decent weather forecast, one last day on the water sounded good to Tina. And better than watching her business being swept away. "Max and I can go out tomorrow if Jenny can come down to the hardware store and spell us."

Charlie's face brightened, and when Jenny saw that, she agreed wholeheartedly. "I'd be glad to get out of this house for a little bit," she declared. She sent Charlie a teasing smile. "I think Dad is tired of me fussing over him, so he'd be relieved to have me gone, and I'd get to see how things are going at the store."

"It's a date." Max met Tina's gaze across the table and grinned, and she had no trouble reading that smile or the double entendre of his word choice. "Me. Tina. Worms. And a boat."

"Good." Jenny met Charlie's smile with one of her own. "Then we can have a nice fish fry on Saturday night. Unless you're too tired to have a crowd around, Charlie?"

"Not if there's fish on the menu," he declared, and for just a minute he sounded like the Charlie of old. Strong. Determined. Decisive.

Tina met Max's eyes across the table and read the "gotcha" look he aimed her way. She couldn't wiggle out of a fishing date with Max, not with Charlie's hopes up.

And the thought of hanging out with Max on the water, handling smelly worms and flapping fish, could prove interesting. Tina was at home in two places: a kitchen and a boat. So if Max thought he was being altruistic by going fishing with her, he had a lot to learn. She might have messed up in the old boyfriend department, but when it came to fish, Tina Martinelli knew her way around Kirkwood Lake.

The unseasonable warmth tempted multiple boats onto the late-season water the next day, anglers wanting one last spin before packing things up for the winter.

Temptation wasn't goading Max into the boat. Love for his father was. He gassed up the motor, checked the anchor and loaded supplies. Fishing poles, bait, tackle, life jackets, compass, a cooler for fish and one for sandwiches, and a thermos of coffee.

He eyed the lake, appraising.

He didn't fear the water after losing Pete. He hated it. Big difference. But the only way to make his father's fish fry a reality was with fish. And there weren't too many jack perch hanging out on shore. He tucked two flotation devices beneath the backseat, and wished he'd thought to do the same before Pete and Amy went cruising that night.

If they'd been sober, with the right equipment, would they be here now, living life?

His heart ached, but his mind went straight to God. *I know what I need to do, Lord. I'm not shirking this confrontation, I'm just busy with stuff on this side of the lake. I'll make it a point to go see the Sawyers once things are settled with Dad. And the store. And the lighting gig. And if anyone tells You that small towns don't come with their own share of drama, well, they're wrong. But I'll go see Mary and Ray. Soon.*

Tina's approach pushed his thoughts into actions.

"We could have used my boat." She settled onto the seat of Charlie's much bigger rig and made a face at Max. "It's not the size of the boat—"

"It's the heart of the fisherman," Max finished one of Charlie's favorite sayings, but went on, "That didn't stop Dad from buying this, did it?"

"Well, with a crew like yours, I suppose a bigger boat could be deemed a necessity."

Max eased the boat away from the dock, turned it around and headed toward deeper water. "But here is where I give in to your expertise. I know the big perch usually seek deeper water in fall, but do you know any hot spots?"

"Warrenton Point with today's breeze, at the end of the longest docks. If not there, then the off side of the west curve, just north of Kirkwood Lodge."

"She can talk the talk," Max teased as he aimed for Warrenton. "But can she back up the talk with action?"

"Time will tell."

He revved the motor, steering the boat through open water. As they drew closer to the point, Max decreased his speed, then idled the engine. His intent was to have a successful trip for his father.

Fish weren't always cooperative and that was a reality every fisherman faced, but today the fish were fighting to be caught.

They brought in eighteen good-size jack perch in the first forty minutes, evenly split. "I will never cast an aspersion about your fishing abilities again," Max noted as he reeled in number eighteen. "I forgot how nice this can be when you troll into a good school of fish."

"Not much time for fishing in the army?"

What should he say? The truth, that he avoided the water purposely? No. "Lack of time, lack of desire." He stared out across the lake, looking at the long, sweeping curve of the west shore, but seeing Pete's face. Hearing Pete's laugh. He sighed. "And busy working my way up. That didn't leave too much time to kick back and do much of anything, actually."

"Those captain's bars say you've done all right," Tina noted as she shifted her line to the other side of the boat. "And it can't be easy to give that all up. Doesn't it become ingrained? The love of adventure, the joy of service?"

"It does." Max rebaited his line, then cast it toward the docks on the opposite side of Tina's rod. "But I faced a few enemies these past few years that wanted me dead. And I decided it would be a shame to have that happen when I'd never been gutsy enough to move outside of my military comfort zone."

Outside his military comfort zone? Tina frowned as she studied a slight shift in the wave patterns.

"Most people don't describe hand grenades, snipers, IEDs and long desert tours as comfort zones. Doing so either makes you odd or oddly exciting." Tina paused and adjusted the angle of her rod. "And I'm not exactly sure how to classify you yet, so I find that more than a little disturbing. An unusual predicament for me."

His smile rewarded her. "I think I like disturbing you, and let's just say when you do a job well, it's easy to get caught in a rut. I wanted to change things up. When Mom called me about Dad's diagnosis, I realized I might be running out of time, and that was stupid on my part."

"They don't think you're stupid." Tina left enough bite in her tone to let Max know she wasn't quite as convinced.

"Well, they love me."

She frowned and reeled her line in as she acknowledged his comment. "They do. And we've fished this out or they've moved off. Let's try the lodge."

"Your wish is my command."

He stowed his line, backed the boat away from the point, then aimed west into the late-day sun. "Gorgeous day."

"And possible snow tomorrow, so it's good we took the time to do this now. I don't ice fish. Not even for Charlie."

"Do you think he's going to make it, Tina?"

The question took her by surprise.

Her heart paused. Her breath caught, because the look Max gave her over his shoulder said he'd read the reality of Charlie's condition and wanted her truthful answer.

She looked off over the lake and shrugged off tears. "No."

Max nodded as if she'd confirmed what he already knew, and Tina realized that despite their close parent-child relationship, he might have trouble discussing this with Jenny. Jenny believed heart and soul that with God, all things were possible.

Tina believed that, too, but she'd watched her parents die, seen her best friend's family suffer through the loss of their son, and she knew that while God wanted his people healthy and happy, the human body was a frail vessel.

Max pulled into a deep-water crevice off the end of the lodge. He stood, turned and grabbed his pole, but not before Tina saw the anguish in his eyes.

She wanted to cry. She wanted to give him hope. She wanted his father to be healthy and happy and ready to rock more grandbabies on his knee, show them how to build a campfire and take them trolling through migrating swans and geese in the boat.

Charlie's timeline said that wasn't likely to happen.

Max pulled himself up. He drew a breath, then slanted her a look that said more than words as he jutted his chin toward her pole. "Let's get this show on the road, woman. These fish won't catch themselves, and there's a bunch of Campbells coming for supper tomorrow night."

His words said he was ready to deal with whatever came his way, as long as Charlie Campbell got his fried perch dinner. Tina figured if the fish didn't cooperate, Max would dive into the water with a net to make sure there was plenty of food. If this was to be Charlie's last perch dinner, Max would see it was a great one. Tina was certain of that.

"Forty-two fish?" Jenny hugged Max and Tina in turn, and Charlie looked suitably impressed when they lugged the cooler full of fish up into the front yard of the Campbell house. "That's amazing."

"Well, our little Tina knows her way around the lake," Max drawled. His grin said he was proud of her, and the combination of Jenny's surprise, Charlie's joy and Max's pride made her feel like she could handle anything. Even in Kirkwood Lake. That realization felt good and surprising all at once.

"I'll clean fish," Max announced, and he set up the old fish-cleaning table that Charlie kept stored in the boathouse. "Do we want to order pizza and wings for supper? I should have these guys filleted and on ice just in time to catch the Thursday-night game. You up for that, Dad?"

"Could be." Was it the sight of the fresh fish or the thought of a football game that brightened his father's eyes? Max wasn't sure, but it felt good.

"I'll turn on the floodlights," Jenny told him. "It's getting dark soon and I don't want you cutting yourself."

"Thanks, Mom."

"I can help." Tina moved over to the small table and pulled up a stool. "I know how to fillet perch."

Max handed her an extra knife. "Don't expect me to say no. There are eighty-four little fillets here, and that's a lot of skin-zipping and slicing."

"It is."

"I'm ordering the pizza to be ready at game time. Is that okay?" Jenny called from the house.

"Perfect. And if some of those wings are Buffalo-style, you'll make me very happy," Max called back.

"Is there another kind, darling?"

Max laughed, because raising five boys and two daughters had schooled his mother on the intrinsic differences. Cass and Addie liked the country-sweet wings with a hint of fire.

The Campbell boys had always tussled for the hotter side of life from early on. Maybe that was what pushed him into the service, the "let's best each other" guy-speak he'd grown accustomed to as a kid.

Now?

He was all right with tough, but he yearned for more. He longed for a chance to be all the things his father had been to him. A kind and giving man, a loving dad, a humor-filled confidant.

"Tina, I ordered hot wings for you, too. With extra blue

cheese. I hope that's okay?" Jenny's voice cut through the thinning light from the far side of the screened porch.

"Perfect. Thank you!"

"Hot wings?" Max sent a look of interest her way as he zipped through the motions of cleaning fish.

"Mmm-hmm."

"Skilled fisherwoman?"

She grinned at the full cooler. "So it would seem."

"And you clean up well."

"I do what I can."

He leaned over, forcing her to look up. Meet his gaze. She did but his proximity made her look nervous. Max decided he liked making Tina Martinelli nervous. And while his head cautioned him to sit back and be quiet, his heart pushed him forward. She sent him a mock-frown as if interrupting her focus was a terrible thing. "What?"

"I think I'm falling for you, Tina. And I'm not too sure what to do about that because you're determined to go and I'm intent on staying."

Her mouth opened. Her eyes went wide, as if the last topic of conversation she expected over a pile of perch was a declaration of affection. A declaration he probably shouldn't make because Max understood the rigors of fall-out, and when folks found out what he did, or rather what he didn't do, people's respect for him was likely to nose-dive. But spending the day with Tina, talking, fishing, trolling the lake for the first time since Pete and Amy's accident...

He felt like he was home, finally.

"You're not like anyone else, you're the prettiest thing ever and your fighting spirit makes me feel like I can fix things. Old wrongs, cranky motors and rusted-out tools."

"Max—"

"Well, now, I didn't say all that to interrupt your work,

and I don't intend to eat pizza and wings while I'm smelling like fish, so we've got to hustle if we're going to have cleanup time, but…" He drawled the last, leaned back in his seat and let his eyes underscore his words. "I just thought you should know."

He'd silenced her.

He decided that might be a good thing to remember for future reference, because strong women like Tina didn't do quiet all that well.

"You don't play fair, Max."

"I thought we ascertained that in the car last night."

Her frown said she remembered their conversation.

"Except I'm ready to be done with war, which brings us back to the first part of the saying."

"And I'm not a game player. Ever. Toying with people's hearts and emotions doesn't make the short list especially since my heart's been run ragged the past few years."

The guard in her tone said she'd erected boundaries for good reason. "Tell me something I don't know." He zip-skinned another fish, like Charlie had taught him years before. "Women tend to be a confusing bunch, if not downright crazy." She bristled and that made him grin. "But not you. And when I asked myself, 'Why is that? What makes Tina Marie Martinelli different?' I knew right off what the answer was. Because she's honest."

She darted a look at him that said he should stop, not go any further.

"Forthright."

"There's a compliment and a half for you."

"Faith-filled."

Her jaw softened. Her eyes did, too.

"And when I'm not with her, she's all I can think about."

Her chin faltered.

Her eyes went wet with unshed tears. "Don't mess with me, Max Campbell." Her voice came out in a tight whisper.

"Two things you should know about me, Tina Marie."

She met his look with her jaw set and her mouth firm, determined and ready to clean his clock if needed. And he decided that riling Tina was a new kind of fun. He liked it, but he held her attention with a straight-on look. "I don't mess with anyone. I talk straight, I shoot straight and I mean what I say every time."

Her throat convulsed, reading his meaning. Hearing his pledge. "And the second thing?"

"I'd like three kids, but I could be talked into four. Under the right set of circumstances, of course."

Her smile started small and grew. She ducked her chin, picked up her filleting knife and growled. "This is how you court a girl, Max? Over a mess of fish and a sharp knife?"

"Whatever works, Tina." He grinned and got back to the fish, but not before winking at her. "Whatever works."

Chapter Seven

Gone.

Tina stared at the vacant lot the next morning, under a cold, leaden sky.

The burned-out shell had been razed and carted away. The concrete deck remained, but the cute garage sale tables and chairs she'd bought, sanded and painted in bright shore-tones of blue, green and yellow had been toted off, as well.

Regret hit her. She'd meant to keep them, to put them in storage, tuck them away. They'd been safe from the fire because they'd been out on the broad, concrete deck. They could have been spared destruction, but she hadn't said anything to the work crew and now they were gone.

Scorch marks marred the concrete, but the lot itself was scraped to the thick cement slab, the footprint of a building she'd loved.

Emotion pushed her forward. The weather had turned seasonal again, with a sharp wind off Lake Erie. Yesterday's transient warmth had been an anomaly, a flashback of Indian summer. Today?

Reality set in. Her business was gone, the lot swept clean and the unseasonable warmth had been jack-knifed east by a Canadian clipper system that promised Thanks-giving snow.

She pictured the jazzy, retro tables she'd stained and stenciled. The fun, mismatched chairs. The cool espresso machine, the bank of syrups. The double-sided deep sink, the rotating convection oven that baked sixteen pies at once. The five-seat counter, small but friendly, and the locals who used to frequent it throughout the year.

"Hey."

Max's voice hailed her.

She turned, fighting the rise of sadness. She wasn't generally overly emotional, but since the fire, it seemed like she couldn't grab hold of her feelings. She didn't like this new normal. It left her vulnerable, an emotion Tina abhorred. "Different, right?"

His gaze appraised her, and his expression changed from wondering to "handle with care."

She made a face and dug her toe into the loose dirt alongside the scraped-clean slab. "I didn't think it would affect me like this."

Max nodded.

"I hated seeing it all burned-out, such a mess, but this seems so final."

"Only as final as you make it, Tina."

Redo? Restart? Begin again? Here?

One look at Max said the idea was tempting. But she wasn't about to jump into rash decisions, not ever again. She hauled in a breath and smiled when he held out a cof-fee. "I thought this might taste good."

"It's morning and it's coffee, so one-plus-one." She paused and sipped, then smiled. "You made me a mocha?"

"Mocha latte. And yes." He slanted the lake a quick look, reminding her of their fishing excursion the previ-ous day. "You've got hidden talents. So do I."

"It's delightful."

"I agree," he said, but he wasn't looking at the coffee cup when he said it.

A slow blush curled up from somewhere around her toes, so she changed the subject. "I wanted to thank you for yesterday." She turned and started walking toward the hardware store. "For using the fishing trip to keep me out of town while they worked here."

He shrugged one shoulder. "I got the girl for the whole afternoon, the first fishing trip I've had in years, and the makings of a great dinner. I was in the winner's circle on all counts."

"You're a thoughtful man, Max."

"I've improved in that department," he corrected her. "And it took a while, but I'm educable, Tina. I do have a shot of bad news, though."

"Charlie?" Apprehensive, she turned quickly and banged square into his arm. He steadied her with his free hand...and then didn't let go.

"No, he's holding his own." He waved west of Main Street to Upper Lake Road with his other hand. "The company that was contracted to do the park lights backed out today."

"No."

His grim expression said yes. "They called the house phone this morning and left a message. I tried contacting them, but got no answer, so I called a guy in Buffalo to check it out. The company bellied-up this week."

"Max." This was the kind of thing that could put the committee over the top. With less than a week to go before the Festival of Lights officially opened how could they possibly fix the situation? "What are we going to do?"

"I'm not sure. The Christmas on Main Street part is all set between the town and the business owners. And the home-owners do their own thing around the lake to give us the circle of light. The living Nativity will be set up for the two weekends before Christmas, with people taking rotations for playing the parts of the family, angels and shepherds in the cold. But the park..." His dark expression said he understood what a huge loss that was to the town fund-raising. "The park drive-through is a big draw and a financial plus for the women's shelter."

"There's got to be someone else to hire."

"Not at this late date," he reminded her. "And if this company dumped a bunch of contracts, then there are other places scrambling for services. I'll check around today, but it doesn't seem likely."

"I can't imagine facing Georgia Palmeteer with this news." Tina matched his frown. "She'll eat us alive."

"We'll keep it to ourselves while I check out other possibilities, but if I haven't come up with something by tomorrow, we'll have to inform the committee," Max replied. "And my dad."

"Do you want me to tell them?"

Max looped his arm around her shoulders, an arm that seemed to know she'd gotten chilled standing at the shore. "No, I'll do it. But first I'm going to see if I can't put some form of Plan B into action. It's always better to deliver bad news with an alternative action plan in place."

"You learned that in the army."

He let go of her, opened the back door of the hardware store, unlocked the inner door and let her precede him as he laughed. "I learned that being Jenny Campbell's son. When your mother's nickname is 'Hurricane Jenny' you grow up realizing she's a force to be reckoned with and act accordingly. Which means unconventional measures became a way of life."

She acknowledged the truth in his words. His mother

had always been the "get 'er done" type the woman folks approached if they needed advice or something accomplished. And Jenny herself was handy with power tools and the softer side of home decor, so her expertise had helped people for decades.

But how were they going to decorate a drive-through park with no Christmas lights?

That posed a tough question with the annual festival looming.

"I asked Mrs. Thurgood to join us tonight," Jenny whispered as Tina hooked her jacket that evening. "She's not as strong as she was last year, and I thought an old-fashioned fish dinner might be nice for her."

"I'll go sit with her," Tina replied. "I miss our wise little chats when she'd come in for coffee."

She purposely hadn't driven to the Campbell house with Max. If she let him drive, he'd have to take her home later, and no way was she setting herself up for more romantic moments. She had enough on her plate right now, didn't she?

I think Max is a pretty nice addition to that plate, her conscience scolded. *You might want to think twice about holding him off. Remember that old window/door thing? When God closes a door, somewhere He opens a window? Why can't that be here? Now? Maybe Max is your destiny and you're too stubborn to see it.*

Max was amazing, she admitted to herself as she crossed the room to see Mrs. Thurgood. But—life was confusing right now. And she didn't do confusing all that well, it seemed.

Because you can't control the confusion, her conscience tweaked one more time. *You like to set the rules, run the show.*

The truth in the reminder made her wince internally.

Let go, and let God. Follow the path. Trust, Tina. That's what it comes down to. Trust.

She'd weigh her internal struggles later, after a night of Campbell fun, a night that might be Charlie Campbell's last fresh-caught family fish fry. No way in the world would she let worry spoil that. She sank down next to Mrs. Thurgood, a sweet old gal who lived in a filled-to-the-brim house outside of town. She reached out and patted the elderly woman's knee. "Mrs. Thurgood, how are you? I don't get to see you all that often now."

The old woman gave her a hug, an embrace that seemed weaker than the last time she'd seen her. "I miss that café! It was like a home away from home, without the clutter, of course. To stop in there or mosey next door to the vintage store and see Carmen and Gianna, well, that just made my day," she exclaimed. "But my driving days are over according to the DMV—though I can't imagine staying cooped up in my place all winter, hoping for a ride to town."

It seemed life's changes weren't just surrounding Tina. Reading the look on the old woman's face, Tina understood that Mrs. Thurgood was facing her own dragons of adjustment. But then Mrs. Thurgood blessed her with a bright smile and said, "I'm thinking of renting that apartment right below you, actually."

"Really?" Tina knew the first-floor tenants in her building had bought a place closer to Clearwater and were scheduled to move. "Mrs. Thurgood, I'd love it if we were neighbors."

"Me, too. It would be just the ticket, I think." Her words said one thing. Her face said she hated the thought of moving. She looked up just then, and her face broke into a wide smile. "Max Campbell. Come give an old woman a hug!"

Max did just that, and the gentle way he embraced their

elderly friend showed the tough, rugged soldier's big heart. "You look wonderful, Mrs. Thurgood."

"Oh, you!" She blushed in delight, and gripped his hands in hers. "It's so nice to have you back, helping with everything. You are a blessing to your family, and this town, and I'm so glad you're here, Max!"

A slight grimace darkened Max's face. Why? Tina wondered. Guilt over being away? Staying away?

But then he smiled and squeezed Mrs. Thurgood's hands gently. "It's good to be home."

"Any luck?" Seth drew a chair up alongside the couch and kept his voice low as he addressed Max. "On the search for lights?"

"No. There aren't lights to beg, borrow or steal in a three-state radius unless we're willing to pay retail and foot the bill."

"Georgia Palmeteer will eat you alive," Seth told him, and in typical brother fashion, he sounded kind of excited about that idea.

"What's gone wrong?" Mrs. Thurgood grasped Max's hand. "What's got you worried about Georgia, Max? Maybe I can help."

Max sent her a rueful look. "Only if you've got a barn full of Christmas lights we can use for the park."

She perked up instantly. "As a matter of fact, I do!"

Seth stared at her.

So did Max.

"You've got Christmas decorations, Mrs. Thurgood?" Tina broke the silence and leaned closer. "I'll help you put them up in your new place if you'd like."

"Oh, no, no, dear, not like that, that's not it at all," the old woman exclaimed. "You know how I can never throw anything away?"

Tina had heard stories about the packed clutter of the old woman's home, but had never visited. "I've heard."

"Well, my husband and son had a thing for Christmas—they just loved it! We collected all sorts of fun things over the years, and George and Butch put everything they had into building great big displays. Once George passed away, Butch kept on buying, right up until he went to war. I didn't have the heart to tell him no," she confessed, "so the barn is chock full of outdoor Christmas decorations. Now, they're kind of old-fashioned-looking, but I'm sure that barn is jam-packed with lots of fun stuff you can use in the park."

Tina looked at Max.

Max returned the gaze.

"If we use Mrs. Thurgood's stash of Christmas lights—" Max began.

"And have people donate any extra lights they may have—" Tina added.

"We can use Dad's emergency backup generators from the store." He looked downright hopeful at the thought. "We might be able to do this, Tina."

"Come out to the house tomorrow," Mrs. Thurgood urged him. "You can use anything you find. If George and Butch were here, they'd be glad I found a home for this stuff at long last."

Max gave her another hug. "I'll do that. Seth, you free tomorrow?"

"No, but Luke is, and there's nothing he'd like better than to help you."

Luke made a face at Seth but shrugged assent as he drew closer. "Count me in as long as Rainey's mother can watch the kids. I'll give her a call."

"Can we do it first thing?" Tina wondered. "Before church, maybe? Because we've got to open the hardware store midday."

"Is there electric in the barn, Mrs. Thurgood? Does it have lights?" Max asked.

She nodded. "Sure does, and far as I know they work fine. I haven't been in there in a good many years," she told them, "so there's maybe the odd critter or two as well, but not too many with a tight roof and no food. Critters like food, so I make sure there's none lying about. An old lady on her own can't be too careful."

From what Tina had heard, careful didn't apply in all aspects of Mrs. Thurgood's life, but the eccentric old woman had been a constant support for Tina's business. She'd shared recipes, insight and time, and her visits to the café had been a welcome respite. "Is 8:00 a.m. good?" She raised an eyebrow to Max.

He nodded. "I'll pick up Luke and meet you there. Mrs. Thurgood, you might have just saved Christmas for the town."

She brightened noticeably. "Well, good! And if Butch was still here, he'd be right alongside you, stringing lights and hanging holly. He loved Christmas so much." She sat forward and aimed her gaze back to Max. "George and I just loved that boy, being our only child and all. When George passed on, it was just me and Butch, getting things done. I didn't want him to join the service, but he had a mind of his own and then I lost him. I lost a part of me that day the army came calling, a part of me that cared about foolish stuff. I decided then and there I'd put folks first, and I've done it, too. My house might be in a sad state of repair, but my soul smiles at the name of Jesus."

Max held her hand. "I believe you." He turned his attention toward the dining room. "Do you feel up to filling your own plate, or can I fill one for you?"

"Since getting up isn't as easy these days, I'd be obliged,

Max Campbell, and I do love your mother's tartar sauce with my fish."

"I'm on it."

Max went to get her food, and Tina bent closer. "You're an amazing woman, Mrs. Thurgood." She gave the older woman's arm a gentle squeeze. "I wanted you to know that."

"Well, thank you, but I'm common enough," she argued lightly. "I do prefer everyday people, though, Tina. The simple folks, the kind I run with. I look at my friend Charlie, there—" she jutted her chin across the wide room "—and I'm just plain sad to see him so ill at his age, but for myself, honey?" She reached a thin-skinned pale hand to Tina. "I won't mind goin' home when the time comes. Seeing my husband. Hugging Butch. It's been a long time gone."

An old mother's lament, but brave and true despite her eccentricities. Tina would miss her bright-eyed initiatives when God called the aging woman home. How blessed she'd been to know her and her quaint wisdom for so much of her life.

"Paydirt."

Luke nodded and sent Max a look of pure surprise the next morning. "It's organized."

"It is that!" Mrs. Thurgood bustled into the sprawling barn after she'd grabbed a mismatched tangle of coat, boots and hat. "The barn wasn't my domain, so I've left it alone. Butch had a nice little apartment over the garage, just the right size for someone on their own, and doing this Christmas stuff for folks was something he and his dad loved. If you look over there—" she pointed to a long group of shelves by the far door "—that's where Butch kept most of the stuff. He had a love for electric from early on, and he took courses in high school at the cooperative place in Clearwater, so he had a fine hand with wiring. 'Course, things were simple back then, not all fancy-schmancy like they have now, but sometimes that simple stuff is more Christmasy than all the electric doodads they've got out today."

"Is that Rudolph?" Luke asked, looking up into the hay loft.

"And all of his friends!" declared Mrs. Thurgood. "With Santa and his sleigh parked on that end." She pointed left of center, and sure enough, Tina spotted a full-size wooden sleigh with a wooden Santa sitting front and center in plain sight, an amazing find.

Max whistled.

Tina grabbed Mrs. Thurgood's arm when the older woman slipped on an uneven surface. "You really don't mind us using this stuff?"

"Mind?" Mrs. Thurgood snorted as if that was the silliest thing she'd ever heard. "Why should I mind? Butch would be sad to think his hard work sat gathering dust all these years. No, you guys load it up and use what you need. I can't say we've got enough for the whole park, but we've got enough to make a difference."

"I'll say." Max slung an arm around the old woman's shoulders and gave her a half hug while he set a plan in motion. "I'll get Dad's trailer and gather all this stuff tomorrow. We'll start rigging the park right away. I can't tell you how grateful I am, Mrs. Thurgood."

"That's what friends are for, Max Campbell." She gave him a big old hug and smiled. "Glad to help."

"Are you as amazed as I am?" Max muttered to Tina and Luke as they approached their vehicles a few minutes later.

"Astonished. I think she's got more than half a park full

of classic Christmas decorations in there, totally vintage and yet timeless," Tina declared.

"Vintage." Max rolled the word around on his tongue, thinking.

"Right." Tina opened her car door and turned. "You know, dated but sweet. An upgrade from *junk*."

"Thanks for the dictionary lesson, but I got that part. I mean, *vintage* is how we can get this all taken care of. We put out a call for any old-fashioned or classic Christmas decorations we can borrow to line the park drive."

"That could work," Luke agreed as he opened the door to his SUV. "If everyone pitches in, we can set up great displays in plenty of time."

"A Vintage Kirkwood Christmas!" Tina grabbed Max's hands. "Max, that might be brilliant."

"Well, it is or it isn't, but knowing we'll have half the park set with Mrs. Thurgood's collection puts me at ease," he admitted. "And I bet the town would get behind something like this."

"Let's notify the committee of the change in plans." Tina ticked off her fingers. "I'll do that so you can focus on planning. I'll put an announcement on Facebook, and I bet Hose Company 2 would let us use their lighted sign to ask for donations."

"I'll call Bill Ripley over at the fire hall, too," Luke said. "Between their ladder truck and the town equipment, we should be able to get this squared away in time for the lighting ceremony Wednesday night."

"Perfect."

Max turned toward Tina as Luke started the engine. He wrapped big, strong arms around her and hugged her close, grinning. "We might have actually nailed this thing. Nice work, Martinelli."

* * *

The slight buzz of an incoming text on his burner phone alerted Max as he climbed the church steps a short while later. The army was contacting him.

He stepped into the anteroom of the church entry, pulled out the phone and scanned the coded message. Rocking to 'Need You Now.' Love Lady A!!!

Translation: You're needed down South.

Max keyed back Concert tickets unavailable.

He was on their payroll for six more weeks. He'd left Fort Bragg knowing he might be called back, hoping it wouldn't happen because his parents needed him here. His commander understood the situation in Kirkwood, and only a serious emergency would push him to request Max's services, which meant if this current situation deteriorated, he could be called into action.

For how long?

That was anybody's guess, but now, with his father's condition, the holidays and his responsibilities here, assuming an instant new identity didn't make the short list. And how would he explain this to Tina? He'd left town once and hadn't returned for ten years. If he disappeared into the night on army business, how would she feel? Would she ever learn to trust him?

A new text buzzed in. Front row filled. Balcony seating options.

Which meant they'd covered the situation for now. But Max knew the drill. With international tensions mounting, anything could happen in that length of time. And probably would.

Chapter Eight

"While I'm very sorry to do this, I'm going to have to withdraw the permission certificate for the drive-through part of the Festival of Lights." Town Supervisor Ron Palmeteer didn't look the least bit sorry when he faced off with Max that afternoon. The self-serving politician seemed oddly confident about the confrontation. Max's guard went on high alert.

"On what grounds?" he asked. His easy tone let Ron be the instigator, a practiced tactic.

The store was busy, but nothing Tina and Earl couldn't handle for a few minutes, and having the rug pulled out from under this long-established Christmas project wasn't something Max would leave unchallenged.

The supervisor kept his voice low, as if hoping other customers wouldn't hear, but the well-heeled bully wasn't going to get his way on Max's watch. Not if Max could help it. "In order for me to sign off, we'd need a licensed electrician to lay out the schematic and oversee the displays."

"And what else?"

Palmeteer frowned. "I think that's quite enough, don't you? With just a few days to get ready, there's no way your hodgepodge of donated lights can handle six weeks of wear and tear. Your father's expertise wasn't lost on any of us, but with him out of the picture, and the contracted company pulling out, we've got to let the park thing slide."

"Oh, I think we'll be okay." Max kept his voice at normal volume. His father had told him enough about the supervisor to suspect the man's motives weren't exactly altruistic. Ron had led a drive to access the lakefront property owned by McKinney Farms, just west of the village. His ploy failed, but revealed his true colors: the supervisor wanted Kirkwood to become more upscale and exclusive, a getaway destination spot geared toward the financially secure. For the moment, Ron was in charge, but Max wasn't about to let him mess with the town's sweet devotion to Christmas. Not if he could help it.

The town supervisor sputtered. His reaction drew curious shoppers closer.

"We won't be okay," hissed Ron. His eyes narrowed. His jaw went tight. Clearly he came into the store ready to do battle. But why? Max wondered.

Charlie and Jenny entered the hardware store just then.

Palmeteer's dark expression said the supervisor hadn't been able to muscle Charlie Campbell about anything, ever, but he wasn't above trying to gain leverage on Charlie's son. Well, that wasn't about to happen.

"Charlie! How are you doing?"

The customer's greeting stalled the Campbells' progress, but realization broadsided Max. His sick father was about to walk into a confrontation he knew nothing about and it was all Max's fault for not telling him about Holiday Lighting's demise.

"Hanging in there," Charlie replied with practiced ease. "I just wanted to swing by and see how things were going while Jen does some rearranging upstairs. Then Beeze and I are heading home for the afternoon." Jenny kissed his cheek before she hurried upstairs to the housewares shop. As soon as she did, Charlie moved beyond the stairway and faced Ron and Max, his face grim. "Problem?"

Max shook his head. "Nope."

"Yes."

Charlie gave the supervisor a look that said he'd wait him out, but not with any level of patience.

"Your son takes casual regard in brushing off fire code. Fortunately for the welfare of the populace, we take it much more seriously at the town offices."

Charlie turned to Max and hooked a thumb at Palmeteer. "You got any clue what he's talking about?"

"The park lights for the festival."

"From Holiday Lighting in Buffalo?"

Palmeteer whistled lightly between his teeth. "You didn't tell him? The entire committee knows that Holiday left us high and dry, but you didn't bother telling the committee chairperson?"

Max ignored the supervisor and faced his father, but the look on Charlie's face showed disappointment. Disappointment in Max? In the situation? Probably both, deservedly.

He waded in. "Holiday backed out of their contract two days ago. They filed for bankruptcy and protection, so the money for the down payment on their services was lost. I waited to tell everyone—" he shot a dark look at Ron Palmeteer "—because Tina and I wanted to come up with an alternative plan. Which we did this morning. Mrs. Thurgood and others have donated a hefty supply of vintage Christmas lights and decorations for us to use in the park. We'll start setting them up tomorrow."

"We *won't* do that because we have no certified electrical contractor on-site," the supervisor countered.

"Chad Bartolo is certified, and he works for the town. I'm sure he'd be glad to—"

"Not gonna happen," declared Ron, looking pleased to

shoot down the idea. "There's no money in the budget to pay overtime for frivolity. The town council would laugh me out of a job if I approved something like that."

Charlie's face went tight, and Max figured the supervisor was lucky that Charlie Campbell was a man of peace. "I'm not dead yet, and if the job needs overseeing, I'll do it," Charlie announced. "We aren't canceling the park. The kids love it and people come from all over to see it. And you know the Clearwater Women's Shelter counts on the money we raise. It's crucial for them."

"Your health won't allow you to oversee weeks of an outdoor lighting display." The supervisor stressed the word *health*, as if Charlie needed any reminding, but when Charlie opened his mouth in rebuttal, Max held up a hand.

"He won't need to. I'm here."

Palmeteer sighed, loud and overdone, as if he had better things to do than stand around and argue with simple laborers. "As I said—"

Max flipped open his wallet and withdrew a card. "If the U.S. government allows me to oversee multimillion-dollar projects, I expect they'll okay me to cover six weeks of Christmas park duty."

"Well, I—" Palmeteer backtracked, clearly at a loss.

"The number's right there." Max pointed to the lower right side of the card. "I'm sure they'd love to talk to you."

The stout, middle-aged man huffed, tossed the card onto the counter and strode out of the store, leaving looks of interest in his wake.

Max turned to Charlie, wishing he'd said something sooner. "Dad, I'm sorry. I should have told you."

Charlie glared at him, and Max couldn't remember the last time his father had looked that angry. Charlie turned and walked out through the back of the store without a word, leaving Max to deal with customers.

Jenny came into the front of the store a few minutes later. "I was upstairs for ten minutes and the world imploded. What happened?"

"I messed up. Big-time." He explained the situation to his mother. When he got done beating himself up, she gave him a big hug, but it didn't help much. He'd come home to help his father, and managed to insult the best guy on the planet by keeping this from him. "I can't believe I did that."

"Max, you stumbled into the middle of an ongoing tug-of-war between the people who would like to see Kirkwood Lake become a go-to resort area for Buffalo and Erie, and those that like the eclectic mix we've enjoyed for a century. Most folks at this end of the lake like our mix of rural, vacation and tourism, and don't want to upset that balance with high-scale development. Your father and Ron don't see eye to eye, and you happened to be in the middle of it."

"I should have told him, though." Max had read the look on his father's face, the expression that said he was tired of being protected and overlooked. And after forty years as a leader in this end of the county, he was right. Max should have gone to him first.

"Max, this is a Christmas lights display, not a peace treaty." Jenny's expression said he should go easier on himself. "Let's be sensible here. Yes, your father wants to know everything that's going on, but if we forget something or don't want to worry him, he'll deal with it. I'd rather have him focused on getting well and gaining strength than wrangling with Ron Palmeteer."

"Well, that's because you're trying to protect him, too." Max wasn't sure if his mother's blessing counted for very much right now, because Charlie got annoyed with her attentiveness on a semi-regular basis.

Jenny sighed, glanced around the now-quiet store and

faced Max. "They say there are stages you go through when you fight a tough diagnosis and prognosis like Dad's."

Max swallowed hard, not sure he wanted to hear this but knowing he needed to pay attention.

"Acceptance is the last stage. Dad hasn't gotten there yet."

"But he seems so calm." Max mentally drew up the times he'd shared with his father over the past few weeks, and while Charlie seemed tired and worn from the treatments, he hadn't seemed overly stressed.

Because he's protecting you. He's protecting everyone. Like he's always done, advised Max's conscience. *Putting others first has always been his motto. It's what makes him Charlie.* "He's pretending to be calm so we don't worry."

"Yes." Jenny put her hand on his arm, the hand that bore a wedding ring from over forty years before. "But part of that pretending is to still feel like he's in charge of something, and he's lost the chance to run the store, run the festival, run his life." She made a face of dismay. "Your dad is used to running things, helping folks, being sought after for advice. To suddenly have everything taken away because he's fighting for his life seems wrong to him."

"So to have us going overboard being nice isn't in his best interests."

"Exactly."

"I'll talk to him tonight. And maybe he can help me plan some kind of schematic for this whole park thing. He's got an eye for it. I don't."

"But Tina said you flashed that card at Ron as if you were some sort of electrical genius."

Max shrugged as he slipped the card back into his wallet. "I can find my way around a fuse box as needed."

Jenny stared at him, then pointed a finger toward the wallet as he tucked it away. "What kind of card was that, Max?"

Max grinned. "A special one."

"And if Ron had taken the number and called?"

"He'd have been told that my electrical expertise has been essential to the safety of the country."

"And if someone called them about excavating a bridge?"

"They'd find out that my bridge-building expertise was essential to the safety of the country."

Jenny studied him, his face, his gaze, and then she grabbed him into a hug, a hug that said she was happy to have him home. "What exactly have you been doing all these years, Max?"

He returned the hug and whispered, "Whatever they asked me to do, Mom."

She held him long seconds before letting him go. She lifted an armload of light boxes she wanted for a Country Cove display and moved toward the stairs. Halfway there she paused. Looked back. "You hang on to that card, you hear? A card like that can come in real handy, son."

She was right. There'd been many a time when someone called that number to check on Max's story, and the caller was always reassured that Max was exactly who they needed him to be.

So far, the army's strategy had worked well. Max wanted that to hold true in his hometown, because no matter what else happened, Max was getting those Christmas lights up and running. And hopefully Uncle Sam wouldn't need him before that happened.

A few hours later, as he pulled into his parents' driveway, he spotted a lone figure standing on the shoreline. Tall and broad-shouldered, Charlie faced the lake he'd known all his life, his bald head covered by a snug winter hat, his arms crossed. He turned, saw Max approaching and shifted his attention back to the water. Max had never seen his father look this sad, this aggrieved before, as if joy itself had been sucked out of him.

"I'm sorry, Dad." Max stepped in front of the man who'd taught him so much, the father who exampled the very best way of being a man, honor bound and family-oriented, and met his gaze. "I messed up and I won't do it again."

Charlie's mouth went tight. "You didn't mess up." His voice was gruff, almost harsh, totally unlike the Charlie Campbell Max knew so well. "You're doing just fine, and I shouldn't take my frustration out on you. Or your mother, or your brothers, or—" He paused, looking beyond Max, his expression seeking, then he pressed his lips into a firm line and brought his attention back to Max. "I'm dying."

Max's heart gripped. His throat went tight. For the life of him, he couldn't muster words past the sudden lump in his throat, and he couldn't look his beloved father in the eye and pretend, so he stood perfectly still and blinked an acknowledgment.

"And I'm not sure how to handle that," Charlie continued. He waved a hand at his body. "All the pills, the IVs, the treatments. They're stopgaps, Max, ways to gain me some time, time with you." He smiled at Max and in that smile, Max saw the first glimmer of acceptance in his father's eyes. "And your brothers and sisters. Time with the kids. I just didn't expect this to come so soon."

"We never do."

Charlie nodded. "That's right. And I don't know what to say, what to do, how to help your mother."

"Can't that be our job?" Max supposed. "After all you guys have done, I think it's okay to let us step in. Take a turn."

"I'm willing enough to share the tasks, but seeing Mom bustling around, all full of hope, trying to keep me on the straight and narrow so I get better..." He hauled in a deep breath, his forehead creased. "I don't think I'll be getting better, Max, but I'm scared to let her down."

"You've never let me down, Charlie Campbell, not one day in your life, so if you've got something to share with me, I expect you to do it." Jenny's voice made them both turn, and the look on her face, the raw acceptance, told Max it was time to slip away.

"I'll leave you guys to settle this, but I want to tell both of you that God couldn't have sent me better parents." He faced them, knowing he'd been blessed beyond belief, and maybe far beyond what he deserved. "If I knew where my birth mother was, I'd send her a thank-you note for dumping me because God put me here, with you guys, and all the craziness of being a Campbell, and I—" Max stepped forward and embraced them both in a hug, a hug that filled Jenny's eyes with tears and made Charlie look damp-eyed, too "—will never be able to repay all you've done for me. For us." He jutted his chin toward the house that sheltered seven kids, four born to be Campbells, three brought by the grace of God. "I love you guys."

He left them to sort through the emotion of the moment. Charlie's acceptance and Jenny's awareness.

His heart crushed at the thought of losing his father, a town patriarch, the man whose kindly example and strong stance said so much. A man of faith and vigor, who knew how to apply both to life. But it was also strengthened by that example, the pledge of a man who saw a job and completed it to the best of his ability. Always.

And that was a quality Charlie Campbell passed on to Max.

Early the next morning, Jenny handed Max a steaming mug of coffee. "Before you say anything or offer an argument, I'm working at the store today," she announced in her "don't argue with me" signature voice. "Jack and Kim are bringing the boys down from Buffalo. They're going to cut a Christmas tree at Wojzaks Farm, then hang out with Dad. You're going to be tied up stringing lights in the park all day, so I'm working with Tina and Earl."

"Perfect."

She stared at him, then laid a cool hand against Max's forehead. "No fever."

"Nope."

"Headache?"

He smiled, remembering her old game. "No, I'm fine. Just ready to let you live your life the way you should. I probably should have realized that as soon as I got back home."

She accepted that, hugged him and ruffled his hair. "I figured you'd catch on sooner or later. And if Dad shows up at the park to help…"

"Close my mouth and let him."

"Bingo. You're a quick study, Max Campbell."

"After a while, things start to sink in. Seth and Luke are helping in the park. We've also got a bunch of guys on the committee and two from the Highway Department."

"Ron Palmeteer approved that?"

"They took vacation days so they didn't need to get approval," Max told her. "Just a group of guys wanting to get something done. We're meeting at nine."

"And I'm ordering Chinese for supper tonight, enough for everyone, so we'll have a big old Campbell supper."

She was turned toward the sink so Max couldn't see his mother's face, but her voice hitched on the last word. He knew that choked sound meant tears.

Max didn't want to look, because as strong as his father was, Jenny Campbell was the driving force behind this family. And in all the years he'd known and loved her, she'd never fallen apart. Oh, she'd cried now and then, mostly when she was spittin' mad or watching some sappy movie she'd seen half a dozen times before, but she rarely caved.

The crack in her voice said she was caving now. Max stepped up behind her. Stubborn, reminding him of another woman he knew, she kept her chin down, as if buttering a bagel had taken on momentous importance.

He put his hands on her shoulders. "Hey."

The shoulders shook.

Max turned her around and drew her into his arms, a role reversal that felt wrong and right all at once. "Hey, it's okay."

"None of it's okay," she whispered, and the harshness of her tone surprised him. "He's insisting on coming into town for the lighting ceremony on Wednesday. The doctors said no crowds, don't risk infection, and he's willing to ignore all that, the stubborn old coot." She sniffled. He glanced around hunting for tissues, saw none and grabbed a paper towel for her. She blotted her face and waved the toweling around. "I know why he's doing it. I know he's facing choices, choices I have to let him make, but I feel so helpless. I question everything I do. Part of me wants to break down, the other part wants to beat up on someone, and I can't fall apart because he needs me to be strong and stoic."

"You're the definition of *strong*, Mom." Max hugged her tighter. "But it's okay to want to beat on something now and again. With a houseful of boys, I think it's a family tradition, right up there with mistletoe and eggnog from McKinney's Dairy store."

"Oh, Max." She hugged him, blotted her eyes and blew her nose, then scowled. "I'm sorry. I shouldn't have dumped on you, it's just the thought of trying to act normal when nothing's normal…"

"Death is as normal as birth," Max reminded her. "Just not as celebrated."

She looked up at him, considering his words, then patted his cheek. "You've done all right, Maxwell."

"I had help." He leaned down and kissed her cheek, wishing he could make this better, knowing he couldn't. And on that note— "Mom, you know I'm not really out of the army until the first of January, right?"

"Yes."

"And there's always the possibility they may call me if necessary."

"They need you, Max?"

"Not at the moment," he hedged. "But they warned me they might."

She moved closer and studied him. "Are you sure about leaving the army? Are you doing this because of our situation here, or because you're ready to move on?"

"Both. So the timing is perfect. But I can't turn my back on a command if it comes."

"So if you disappear in the dark of night..."

"Know that I'll wrap it up and get back here as quick as I can," he promised. "Because this is where I want to be."

She reached out and hugged him, hugged him hard. "I love you, Max. I've loved you since that day we picked you up at Social Services and brought you home."

"You gave me cinnamon rolls and hot chocolate and let me try eggnog that first Christmas, and it's been a love affair ever since." He hugged her back. "Thank you for coming for me that day. For saying yes when that phone call came saying they had a little boy waiting."

"Timing," she assured him with a smile. "Luke had just moved into his own room and having a noisy little brother to pester him helped to keep him humble. It was the least I could do. Do you want a bagel before you take off?"

He shook his head as he grabbed his to-go cup of coffee. "I'll catch food later. We're supposed to get rain tonight, so if we nail this park setup today, I can relax with Dad a little. That ranks higher than stringing lights in trees."

"I'll see you tonight. I love you, Max."

He smiled from the door. "Feeling's mutual."

Tina parked her car just south of where the light crew was working, opened her back hatch, stuck two fingers into her mouth and gave a sharp whistle. Seth Campbell turned first. "You've done that ever since you were a kid."

She laughed as she withdrew a large drink tray filled with steaming coffees and hot chocolate. "Warm drinks, guys. Break time."

She didn't have to tell them twice. And when she pulled out a box filled with sandwiches, chips and a box of her fresh-baked cookies, the words of approval made the expense and time worthwhile.

"Tina, you rock."

"I owe you, Martinelli."

"You want flowers this spring, I will come and plant you a garden, Miss Tina!" Bert Conroy held up his ham-and-swiss on grilled rye and grinned. "This is one happy landscaper right now."

Tina glanced around and tried to not look like she was hunting for Max, but Luke laughed at her. "Max had to run to Dad's store for a few things. Or to check out the pretty girl working there. You must have just missed him."

She almost pouted, and if there was one thing Tina Marie Martinelli never did, it was pout. But knowing she'd missed Max by a hair while she was ordering sandwiches at the deli made her almost succumb.

A car engine cruised up the road behind them, and when

Tina turned, Max was pulling into the parking space south of hers. His grin?

Wonderful.

The look in his eyes that said he was happy, surprised and quite possibly downright delighted to see her?

Better yet.

Their eyes met. Locked. And stayed locked.

"Aw, look how cute they are." Luke made a gagging noise. Total guy.

"Hey, it wasn't that long ago that you were doing the same thing," said Seth, "so I'd zip it if I was you."

"Look who's talking," countered Luke.

"Except I'm not the one teasing a guy who's packing heat and highly skilled in combat maneuvers," Seth shot back. "Which makes me the smart one. Or should I say still the smart one. Not like that's a big surprise."

The guys laughed, and when Max walked over and grabbed Tina in a big hug, they hooted approval.

"Max."

"My way of saying thank-you for the sandwiches," he told her as he reached into the box. "I'm excited to see food. And you."

"You said food first. I could take offense."

He waved his wrapped sandwich toward the gathered men. "Audience intimidation. The pretty girl is always first."

"Any pretty girl?" she asked out loud.

This time he stopped, faced her and smiled. "Nope. Just one."

She blushed as the guys groaned, then she smiled up at him, reading the emotion behind his fun words, seeing the warmth and camaraderie. He grabbed a coffee eagerly, added cream and sugar, and snugged the lid down before sipping it. "Perfect. And I knew you were doing this because my mother ratted you out. She thought it was funny and not exactly a surprise that you came here mid-day, while, in *her* words—" he stressed the pronoun for emphasis "—I was making an excuse to stop by the hard-ware store and see you."

"Great minds think alike." Looking up, she found her-self lost in the depths of his dark brown eyes, the didn't-bother-shaving-to-work-in-the-woods-rough chin and the hint of curl returning around his neckline.

"They do." He chucked her on the arm, noted the time and wolfed his sandwich in record time. "Channel Seven says the rain's moving in by four, and I want all systems checked and ready to roll before then. And—"

A noise interrupted him.

His attention shifted to the southern end of the park road. He turned, caught Seth's eye and called Luke's name softly. His brothers followed the direction of his gaze and watched as Charlie and their oldest brother, Jack, pulled up in Jack's SUV. Dressed in outdoor work attire, the two Campbell additions came ready to help.

Mixed emotions ruled the moment, until Seth tossed his coffee cup into the trash bag Tina brought, strode forward and gripped his father's hand in a firm show of support. "Now we'll get something done!"

Charlie grinned.

Jack's face said he was just doing what he was told, and Luke and Max moved forward in welcome.

Tina shifted her attention to the other workers.

Their expressions told a story of empathy and under-standing, but not one of those burly guys made a big deal about having Charlie on-site. No, sir, they shouted out wel-comes as if it was any old day, asked advice and then got back to the business of decorating a town park.

An artist might have been able to capture the rare combination of broad emotions of those precious moments, but Tina was no artist, so she pulled out her cell phone to record the moment. The Campbells, making the best of a rough situation, like always.

"Hey, you're not dressed for this damp chill." Max motioned her toward the car. "And if my father catches you sloughing off on company payroll, he's liable to get upset."

Charlie laughed and moved down the road at a steady pace. "Let's see what you've got here. If we can get this hodgepodge of lights looking like something decent before the end of the day, I'll sleep well tonight."

"Me, too." Max waved to her but stayed by his father's side, attentive to Charlie's advice. Tina raised her phone and snapped a series of pictures, the Campbell boys walking with their dad, all eyes turned on him, soaking up his wisdom.

It would be a day to remember. A day to cherish, and her pictures would help re-create the memory.

She climbed into the car, turned it around and headed to the village below. The town's efforts might not have the grandeur a professional lighting crew would have supplied, but little kids wouldn't notice any of that. All they'd see were lights, bright lights, twinkle lights, chaser lights. And they'd be happy.

With Thanksgiving three days away, and the circle of lights slated to blink on at dusk on Wednesday, having this job done would mean kudos for Max and the Campbells.

And the look of satisfaction on Charlie's face, to work with four of his sons at one time?

Priceless.

Chapter Nine

Go time.

Max and Bert Conroy had run a preliminary light test midafternoon. They'd held their breaths, thrown the switch and the world did not implode. *Then.*

Now, if they got the same result tonight, when the village and shoreline blinked on around five-thirty, he'd breathe a whole lot easier. And if nothing major went awry in the next six weeks?

Max might consider doing this again next year.

"I made you coffee." Tina clamped a lid on his to-go cup, then slipped into her heavy coat. "Two sugars, two creams."

"I like having my own personal barista. I could get used to this." He smiled across the top of the cup and when she rolled her eyes at him, he glanced around. "Where's yours?"

"No time, I'll get one later. You've got to be—"

"Here." Max took a sip of the coffee, then handed her the plastic travel mug. "We'll share."

"We will not."

He made a face at her. "You'll have supper with me, but you won't share my coffee? That's ridiculous, Tina."

"I'm simply abiding by our nonfraternizing rules. So should you."

"I believe I already cited the impossibility of that. And besides—" he waited until she looked up "—the army saw to it that my skill set is breaking rules. Which brings us back to the 'all's fair in love and war' discussion."

"I'm not discussing any such thing," she chided. "And we need to get over to the town square, ASAP. Once Reverend Smith is done with the prayer service, you've got to be ready to hit the switch. You can't be late. You're, like, the vice-president in charge of Christmas lights, a VIP around here during the holiday season."

"I'm not going without you. And don't worry, I've got it covered. Make your coffee. It only takes a minute."

"Which is about what you have," she grumbled, but she brewed a quick cup, fixed it and snapped a lid on tight. "Okay. We're good to go."

He held the door open, locked it behind her, then let her precede him down the front steps.

The street and the white-frosted green milled with people. Old, young, tall and small, the diversity made this lighting ceremony a wide-ranging event. He reached out and grabbed Tina's free hand when he descended the steps, then tugged her around the back way, behind the church. "This gains us some serious leverage because fighting through that crowd would mean talking to folks, and we're skating close on time as is." They moved across the back church parking lot, through the lower end of the cemetery, then into the park square opposite Seth's house. "Done, with ninety seconds to spare."

"Not bad." She sipped her coffee and smiled up at him. "I'm impressed, soldier."

He started to smile, but Ray and Mary Sawyer approached from one side, with Sherrie and her husband,

Jim, behind them. From the other side of the street, Seth and Gianna worked their way across the green with Charlie and Jenny. Seth carried Bella, bundled from head to toe in a bright pink fleece snowsuit with teddy-bear ears. Mikey was dressed in a brown version, but he stubbornly kept grabbing his hood and yanking down, giving his petite mother a hard time. Seth's adopted daughter, Tori, and Carmen Bianchi flanked Gianna, and the sight of his brother's growing family and the Sawyers drove the sharp difference home.

Seth was here with his family, a spirit of joy abounding.

Pete would never have that chance.

"Max! Tina. We're so excited about all this." Mary grinned up at Ray, then added, "The thought of a new baby, our first grandchild, Christmas, the lights..."

"Grandson," added Ray, clearly proud. "Peter James Morgan, named for his Uncle Pete—"

Max's heart strangled.

"And next year this time, little Pete will be here with us." Mary pressed a kiss to Sherrie's cheek, clearly delighted. "I'm just crazy excited to think of it!"

Nearly fifteen years they'd waited for this new chance at happiness. Fifteen years without their oldest son. A decade and a half of an empty chair, Pete's laugh silenced by an early grave.

Guilt clutched Max and refused to let go.

Why hadn't he said something? Why had he stormed off, letting Pete make the final decision?

You know why. You didn't want to be a third wheel, and you felt like Pete would rather be alone with Amy than have a buddy hanging about, especially a buddy that didn't want to drink with them.

Reverend Smith keyed his microphone. The gathered crowd went quiet, waiting.

The reverend smiled at the crowd, letting his gaze wander and linger here and there. When he got to the growing group of Campbells and Sawyers, he paused. Not a long pause, but enough to tell Max that the aging rector recognized the moment.

He knows. Or at least suspects. And why wouldn't he? Max realized. The reverend had officiated at Pete's funeral. He'd watched Pete and Max grow up, he knew their families, their friends. Maybe ministers came especially equipped with guilt meters, or as least a heightened awareness of human reactions.

The reverend looked at him, straight at him, and his gentle gaze said the time was right, the time was now.

But then he launched into a sweet story of Christmas, of Christ as light. With the wind unpredictable, each person had brought a penlight or a cell phone with a flashlight device, and when the reverend called for them to turn on their little lights, hundreds of tiny beams filled the night.

"You've heard it said that it is better to light one candle than to curse the darkness." The reverend motioned toward the sprinkling of lights surrounding the decorated gazebo in the town square. "For the next six weeks, let us make sure our lights, the light of Christ within us, shine as brightly as our town and lake shines during this blessed and joyous Christmas season. And now, may the Lord bless thee, and keep thee: May the Lord make His face shine upon thee, and be gracious unto thee: May He lift up His countenance upon thee, and give thee peace."

A chorus of "Amen" resounded to the old benediction from the book of Numbers, and as Tina nudged Max forward to hit the switch, he balked. Smiling at his father, Charlie Campbell nodded and moved through the crowd.

The doctors had warned Charlie to avoid infection, to stay out of crowds, to lay low, but as his father threaded his way to the gazebo, he paused and shook every hand offered. If this was going to be Charlie's last Christmas in Kirkwood, he seemed determined to make it a good one.

He drew up alongside the reverend, reached out, shook his pastor's hand and then hit the switch.

Main Street was flooded with light; beautiful, warm, holiday light.

Set to timers, other banks of lights blinked on around them. The village, the circle of homes surrounding the lake, the businesses, all decked out.

And when the park switch was thrown, a collective gasp filled the air.

Vintage yet timeless, the depth of light along Park Drive would thrill every carload of people who came to see the beautiful displays.

"Amazing." Tina hugged Max's arm and smiled up at him.

"I'm pretty psyched that it all came together," he admitted.

She shook her head. "Not the lights, although I have to say I think they're the best ever. You, Max. You're amazing."

She meant it. He read the truth of her emotions in her eyes, the smile she aimed at him. And despite what he needed to face once and for all, Tina's shining approval made it feel possible.

The crowd didn't linger long. A brisk west wind promised deepening cold and most likely snow by morning, but as folks headed home, greetings of the season echoed around him, making him feel like he could handle anything, anything at all.

Even the truth.

"Uh-oh."

Max followed the direction of Tina's gaze and paused a few minutes later. "Uh-oh, what? I don't get it."

"The restaurant." She indicated the people heading toward The Pelican's Nest. "Look at the stream of people going in there."

"That's bad?" The confusion in his voice said he wasn't following her, but then Max had never worked in the food industry. A rush like this, without the proper staff?

Crushing from a restaurant perspective. "I've got to go help them." She darted across the street and moved quickly up the sidewalk to the far side of her parents' old business.

"Me, too."

She ducked behind several cars and turned as she pulled open the back door. "What does a soldier know about restaurants?"

"I can clear tables and do dishes. And you might be surprised by the wealth of things I know, Tina."

"I already am and find it more than a little intimidating," she whispered, then breezed into the restaurant kitchen as if she belonged there.

Laura looked shell-shocked by the growing crowd. Ryan's expression alternated from nervous to strained. Han, the Vietnamese cook who'd worked for her parents years before, looked stressed, as well. Tina tossed her coat onto the pegged rack alongside the back door and grabbed two aprons from the bin. She tossed one to Max and donned the other. "We're here to help. Laura, you want kitchen or tables?"

Gratitude and surprise softened Laura's expression. "I'll help the girls out front. You and Han can cover this. Max, I—"

"Dishes." He moved to the large commercial machine, slid the first filled rack of dishes into place and locked it down. "Uncle Sam makes sure everyone knows how to operate one of these babies."

Laura hurried out. Ryan's worried gaze went from Tina

to Max then back again before he followed his mother into the front of the restaurant.

Han assessed the new situation, grinned and pointed to the stack of orders. "You prep, like old times, eh?"

"Will do."

She bustled around the kitchen, laying plates, starting orders, doling out specials Han had prepared earlier in the day. Wednesday-night pasta specials were a standing tradition in Western New York, and Han had prepped accordingly. Tina prayed that lots of folks would want rigatoni and meatballs tonight. That would take a load of work off the minimal staff.

She put a new kettle of water on to precook more pasta, glanced around, and asked, "Garlic bread?"

Han made a face. "No more."

"No more tonight? Or you don't serve it anymore?"

"No more, anymore. Too much money."

Her father's garlic bread, a Martinelli tradition, the bad-for-your-waistline deliciousness that brought throngs of folks to The Pelican's Nest every Wednesday. Great sauce, al dente pasta and Gino's warm, buttery garlic bread, dusted with fresh basil.

If she was running this place, the last thing she'd drop would be the Italian staples that set the "Nest" apart from other lakeside restaurants. With their family diner atmosphere, steeped in Italian traditions, they'd provided family dining experiences at reasonable cost.

Her parents hadn't gotten rich off the place, but they'd done okay, and shouldn't that be enough?

Rocco's image came back to her, gruff and scowling, grumbling over money and costs all the time. How hard it must have been for Laura to live with him, deal with his outbursts.

Unexpected sympathy welled within her, but she couldn't

dwell on that now. The three waitresses and Laura kept sliding fresh orders onto the wheel, and as Han moved them to the hanging bar over the grill, she'd prep the plate, drop fries or pull potatoes, and let Han finish the order from his spot. Max alternated between rolling dishes through their cycle and cutting fresh lemons and veggies for tomorrow's specials. The old kitchen radio added background inspiration. Old hymns blended with new Christmas carols, the jovial tones adding to the familiar atmosphere.

By eight o'clock the crowd had dwindled to a few dawdling diners, enjoying a few minutes of quiet before going out into the cold.

Laura came into the kitchen, faced Tina and Max and promptly burst into tears.

"Hey!" Tina moved forward, not sure what to do. She looked back at Han.

He shrugged, just as confused.

"Laura, I—"

"Thank you."

Tina paused as Laura grabbed some tissues from a box behind her, mopped her face and took a deep breath.

"Are you okay?"

Laura faced Tina more fully and offered a watery smile. "I'm fine. That's the first time we've been busy like that in over a year. It felt—wonderful!"

"I love a rush," Tina admitted. "The adrenaline gets going, and pretty soon you've got a rhythm of food and orders and checkouts and seating and if all goes well, it's like a well-oiled machine."

"And when it doesn't, chaos erupts." Laura breathed a sigh of relief. "No chaos tonight, thanks to you guys. And you." She smiled at Han, then wrapped Ryan in a hug as he carried another bus pan of dishes into the kitchen. He looked embarrassed and slightly worried, unsure what to make of this kitchen scene.

Tina couldn't blame him. For years he'd been told to avoid her and now she was standing in his mother's kitchen, filling orders. "Great job tonight, Ryan."

He ducked his chin.

Laura looked like she wanted to reprimand him, but Max changed the subject. "So is this the norm? When folks come to town for the lights or the lighting ceremony? Because I'm beginning to see why the light gig is so important if it pumps local businesses like it did tonight."

"Well." Laura shifted a sympathetic look to Tina. "It was always busy during the light festival and the opening ceremony, but it was especially busy tonight because Tina's café is gone."

"True enough." Tina made a face, then sighed. "But I have to say, this was a lot of fun, Laura. Working with Han again. Pumping orders. It felt like old times."

The middle-aged Asian cook grinned. "Is very good, no?"

"Is very good, yes!" Tina laughed at him, sharing an old joke, wondering why it felt so good to work with Han and Laura again.

Sweet memories of what had been? Or longing for what could be?

"Well." She peeled off her apron, tossed it into the appropriate bin and stretched. "I'm heading out. This was fun, and if you need help the next few weeks, Laura, I'd be glad to step in. I'll be right across the street at the hardware store, and if the light show brings folks like it generally does, the extra help might come in handy."

"You'd be over here every night?" Ryan's sharp surprise said he might look like his grandfather, but he had a measure of his father's rudeness.

"Ryan!"

"The busy ones, anyway." Tina kept her voice level and met the boy's frustrated gaze.

"Hey, I'm not the one that called her names and shook his fist out the window for years," Ryan defended himself. "Now Dad's gone and all of a sudden she's like our new best friend? What's up with that, Mom?"

Laura stared at him, mouth open. She started to speak, but he turned and rushed out of the kitchen. The slap of the back door said he was gone.

"Tina, I—"

Tina raised a hand to stop her. "Laura, it's time we all moved beyond the past. I'm sure Ryan heard a lot of stuff over the years. He's young. He'll sort things out in his head soon enough. But in the meantime, you have a business to run and I don't mind helping you. You're my father's sister. He loved you. My mother loved you. And I won't pretend it didn't feel nice—and weird—to be here again." She shrugged. "Can't we just take it a day at a time? I'll come over and help as needed, and we'll all take a breath. Okay?"

"I'd like that, Tina. And if you want to use our ovens for anything—"

"Like pies tomorrow morning?" She'd noticed the empty dessert cooler, and the thought of opening a restaurant on Thanksgiving with no pie seemed alien.

Laura inhaled. "You'd do that?"

"I miss not doing it, so yes. I'll be here by six."

"I'll meet you and make coffee," Laura promised. Her eyes brightened. "Tina, thank you. I don't know what other words to use because *thank you* doesn't seem like enough."

Tina jerked a thumb toward the window, where a side view of the church spire reached up into the trees. "Forgive us our trespasses as we forgive those who trespass against us. I forgot that for a while, Laura. But I won't forget again. I promise."

"I'm so happy." Han grinned but kept cleaning the grill, getting ready for closing time. "I will serve the best turkey tomorrow with the best pie. A true Thanksgiving meal!"

"And while I'd love to wash dishes nightly, I must bestow the honor on someone else, although I hate to miss all the fun," Max teased as he took their jackets off the peg rack and held Tina's out. She started to reach for it, read his droll expression and slipped her arms into the sleeves, allowing him to help her.

And when he rested his hands on her shoulders as if they belonged there?

It felt like they did.

He grabbed his leather gloves and opened the kitchen door. "Laura, Han, it's been real."

Han grinned her way. "Very real with Miss Tina here!"

"Thank you, Max. We're grateful." Laura included Han in her statement, and the Vietnamese cook nodded.

"It is our pleasure to have you back here."

Han's words touched Tina's heart because she felt exactly the same way. It had been a pleasure to jump in, work with Han, run the kitchen she'd known for years.

A thread of hope unfurled inside her.

She paused outside and looked back, studying the lakeside eatery from the sidewalk.

"You missed this place."

"You think?" She turned his way and lifted her eyes to his.

"I *know*." He stressed the verb purposely. "It was written all over you tonight. You jumped in like you belonged there, and watching you work, throwing those orders?" He shifted his attention to the restaurant, then brought it back to her. "You fit, Tina."

"I do." She shrugged, and started to move away. "Well. I did."

He laid an arm around her shoulders, slowing her down. "Still do. You can pretend otherwise, but I know what I saw."

He was right. She knew it the moment she took her place to Han's left, like a dance she'd practiced and performed for years.

Working with Han, hearing the hustle and bustle of the waitresses and Laura, the customers, the clang of dishes as Ryan bussed tables...

She'd missed all that by working alone. The downside of being a one-man band was that you were a one-man band. The flow of a busy, well-coordinated restaurant, like she'd experienced tonight?

That's what she'd been raised to do, and she hadn't realized how much she missed it until just now. "Well, I was raised there."

"There's that," Max mused. "And your inherent kitchen skills. All that baking I've heard so much about—"

"I love baking."

"Can't prove it by me," Max retorted. "We've worked together for over a week and I've seen two measly cookies. Kind of lame, Tina."

She laughed, and it felt good to laugh. They got to her door, and she swung about, surprised. "That's the first time I've passed the café site without getting emotional. I didn't even realize we'd gone by."

"The company, perhaps?" Max bumped shoulders with her, a friendly gesture.

"Indubitably," she joked back, then looked up.

His eyes...

Dark and questing, smiling and wondering.

He glanced down at her mouth, then waited interminable seconds, for what? Her to move toward him?

She did.

Would he ask permission? Would he—

The warmth of his lips gave her the answer. His arms wrapped around her, tugging her close. The cool texture of his collar brushed her cheek, a contrast to the warmth of his mouth.

He smelled like leather, dish soap and fresh lemons, a delightful mingling of scents in the chill of a Christmas-lit night.

Perfect.

Max's singular thought fit the moment.

Holding Tina, working with Tina, kissing Tina?

Perfect.

He pulled her close when they ended the kiss and tried to level his breathing.

No use. Being with Tina meant a ramped-up heart rate and accelerated breathing, which meant being without her, even for a little while, would equate a new low. "Well."

She pulled back, frowning, as if about to scold him, but then she smiled, put her hands up around his neck and whispered, "Do-over."

Like the day they met. *Met again*, Max corrected himself as he languished in one more kiss. When he finally let her go, he dropped his forehead to hers and smiled. "I didn't think we could improve on the first one," he whispered, his forehead warm while the cold air chilled his cheeks. "But amazingly, we did."

Her smile curved her cheeks beneath his. He pulled her into a warm, long hug, the kind of embrace he wanted to enjoy forever. Here, in Kirkwood, with the past behind them and the future ripe with possibilities.

"Go in." He palmed her cheeks with his gloves, smiled and gave her one last kiss. "I'll see you tomorrow. Mom said you're bringing pie for Thanksgiving."

"I am if I can get my mind off kissing you. That might be my morning downfall, Max Campbell."

He grinned wider. "Worth the risk. I can always buy a pie. Finding a Tina?" He raised his shoulders and his eyebrows, hands splayed. "Much more difficult."

He watched her go in, waited for her lights to blink on, then strode to his car parked back at the hardware store.

He had one final coat of paint to apply to the café tables he'd rescued from the fire site before they cleared the mess away. The chairs were done, and the lustrous satin finish said summer in bright tones of yellow, green and blue. The alert from command meant he needed to be ready at a moment's notice. He didn't want anything left undone if he got called to duty.

He started the car, eased away from the building, then paused at the road, considering. He could go straight home and get ready for Thanksgiving when all the family would gather at the Campbell homestead. Or he could head to the far side of the lake and see the Sawyers.

Now? The day before Thanksgiving? Are you nuts?

He swallowed hard.

He'd been called worse. But hearing the reverend tonight, seeing his gaze sweep their families, the thought of possibly being called up and leaving things unsettled much longer gnawed at him.

He turned right and aimed the car for the western shore. He passed Tina's place and pictured her inside the vintage-style rooms.

She'd looked tired and energized tonight, a fun combination, deepened by facing the shadows of her past. Standing in the lighted doorway, kissing Tina, he knew he could do no less.

He pulled into the Sawyer driveway about five minutes later. He got out of the car, shut the door and walked onto their porch. He knocked lightly, hoping they weren't asleep, and when Mary Sawyer came to the door wearing an apron, he realized his foolishness.

No one hosting Thanksgiving got to bed early on Wednesday evening. She swung open the door. "Max! What a surprise, come in! What's happened? Is there something wrong with the light display in the park?"

He shook his head as Ray took his place alongside his wife. "You need help, Max?"

He paused, swallowing hard around the lump in his throat, while two of the nicest people in the world faced him, and said, "I came to apologize for Pete's death. I know it's too little, too late, but I can't see you guys all the time without you knowing the truth. Pete's death was my fault."

Mary's face paled, then crumpled. She reached out a hand to him. "Max, no. It was an accident."

Ray grabbed his arm and pulled him into the living room. "Sit down, Max. What's this all about?"

Altruistic, even at a moment like this, but that shouldn't surprise Max. The Sawyers had raised their children with strength, expectations and loving care. Warmth was their benchmark. He tried again as Mary and Ray sat, facing him. "Pete and I were together that night. Earlier in the evening. I'd come over and then Amy showed up. She'd gotten out of work early and wanted to surprise Pete."

"Right." Mary nodded. "And you went home before they took the boat out. Max, we knew that. Sherrie and Tina saw you before I took them to the amusement park for the reduced ride night."

That wasn't a big surprise. Tina and Sherrie loved to

spy on him and Pete back then, a pair of pesky tomboys, cute and annoying.

The thought of the tough kid Tina was then and the strong woman she'd become pushed him on. "I left because Pete had been drinking. He paid Cody Feltner to stop at the liquor store in Clearwater and hook him up. Cody dropped it off sometime that afternoon. By the time I left to go home, Pete and Amy were already pretty wasted."

He stared down, twisting his hands, then brought his gaze up. "I'm so sorry. I shouldn't have left. I should have called you guys. I should have taken the keys to the boat. I should have done something other than go home mad because my best friend was behaving like an idiot." His throat went tight. Simple breathing was getting harder to do, facing these good people and telling them he could have saved their son and Amy and didn't do it. He hauled in a breath and manned up. Met their eyes. "I came to apologize for what I didn't do that night. If I'd made other choices, Pete and Amy might still be alive. I'm so sorry." His voice cracked. His jaw hurt. "So terribly sorry. Please forgive me."

Ray's face swam before him, an ill-defined image of sorrow and angst.

"Oh, Max." Mary moved forward, knelt before him and took his hands. "Max Campbell, did you think we didn't know that Pete and Amy were drinking? Did you think we blamed you?"

"I—"

"Max, we'd pushed Pete into therapy a few weeks before the accident," Ray told him. "We saw what was happening, and with college coming up, we knew Pete's drinking was out of control. We were scared to death to have him go off to college, with no rules or regulations. He was mad at us for interfering. For weeks we didn't leave him alone in the house. One of us was always here, making sure he didn't drink."

"But that night we knew Amy was working, we knew you were coming over and we'd gotten tickets for the girls to go to Darien Lake," Mary explained. "We'd promised them, and it felt wrong to keep breaking our promises to Sherrie because we had to stand guard with Pete."

Ray rubbed a hand through his thinning hair. "I was on ambulance duty. I got a call for an emergency in Warrenton and Mary had the girls at Darien. Then that call was followed by a second call, and I was gone hours longer than I expected. When I got home, Pete, Amy and the boat were gone."

"Max." Mary wrapped her hands around his. "This wasn't your fault. And it took a long time for us to realize it wasn't our fault, either. Kids don't always make good decisions, and when you add addictions into the mix?" She frowned, her blue eyes clouded with sadness. "We loved our son. We still do. But Pete knew better than to drink like that, he knew better than to take the boat out under the influence, and those two choices led to tragedy. It wasn't your fault."

"But—"

"If you pave life's roads with unanswered questions, you have a real hard time finding the answers, Max." Ray crossed the space between them and sat down next to him. "You've carried this for a lot of years. Too many. And despite Pete's mistakes, I believe God forgives the foolishness of children. I believe I'll see my son in heaven, and that we'll be reunited. We'll gather at the throne of the Most High and be together. But Pete would be the last person to want you to feel guilty. He loved you, in spite of his behavior before he died. And that's the Pete we remember, the one who loved his friends and family before he became an alcoholic."

Max's heart went tight.

Then it loosened.

They didn't hate him. They didn't blame him. They knew about Pete's choices and even with that, Mary and Ray couldn't protect him 24/7.

"There is no forgiveness needed." Mary's firm tone highlighted her words. "We loved you then, we love you now, and we knew how badly Pete's death affected you. But never in my wildest dreams did I realize you lugged this guilt around. Guilt like this isn't of God, Max. God loves. He sees. He knows. He forgives. I don't want you to spend one more minute blaming yourself. Heaven knows such a thing never crossed our minds."

Ray swiped a hand to his eyes.

Mary made no pretense of not crying. She grabbed Max in an embrace that felt good, and long overdue…

"Thank you."

He stood. Mary and Ray stood also, and instead of reaching for his hand, Pete's dad pulled him into a big, long hug. "You're a good man, Max. And I'm proud to know you. And to work with you. And if you settle down here now that you're leaving the service, there will always be a place at our table for you. I hope you know that."

He did. *Now.* He returned the hug, grabbed his gloves and moved toward the door. Almost there, he turned. "I'm sorry for coming so late. I just had to get over here. See you. Talk to you."

"I'm glad you did." Ray clapped a hand to Max's shoulder. "Very glad. I wish we'd had this conversation ten years ago. But at least we've had it now."

"Yes."

A kitchen buzzer alerted Mary to Thanksgiving chores.

She turned, surprised. "I've got pies in the oven. Good thing I set that timer, because I forgot all about them!"

Max gave her one last hug. She patted his face and hurried to the broad kitchen overlooking the lakefront.

Ray opened the door. "Thank you, Max. For being Pete's friend all those years, for being a good soldier, for being on hand now that Charlie needs you. I'm proud of you, son."

He extended a hand to Max.

Max took it, and when Ray Sawyer shook his hand, weight tumbled from Max's shoulders.

They didn't hate him.

They knew Pete was in trouble, and even with their diligence, Pete managed to get hold of alcohol and get drunk.

Foolishness of youth.

Ray's words made sense to Max, now that he was older. He couldn't see that clearly as a teen. All he'd known was the guilt of walking out on his friend, leaving him there with Amy and the bottle.

He paused at the car, looking out over the lake. Clouds had nipped the earlier starlight, but merry lights circled the expanse of water, and the brilliance of the decked-out village called to him.

His father had started this beautiful tradition years ago. He'd spearheaded the committee, the planning and then the implementation, all to bring the joy of Christmas and the light of Christ to people.

Max drew a deep breath, drinking in the beauty of reflected light, and knowing, at long last, he was exactly where he needed to be. Home, in Kirkwood Lake.

He climbed into the driver's seat, backed out of the Sawyer driveway and aimed for the eastern shore. He'd spend tomorrow with his family, surrounded by Campbells and

Campbell friends, sharing the first family-themed holiday he'd allowed himself in over ten years.

And he'd have Tina there, by his side, laughing. Talking. Kissing?

The thought of that made him smile.

He shouldn't feel this way after so short a time. His brain knew that, but his heart wasn't listening. His heart thought being with Tina Martinelli was the best thing that ever happened to him, and now…if he could just get her to hang around a while…he might be able to convince her heart of the very same thing.

And he had every intention of doing just that.

His burner phone buzzed as he pulled the car into his parents' driveway. He walked into the house and read the message. Casting Crowns concert in Erie phenomenal! Faves: Set me Free and East to West. Wish you were here!

His heart sank. He knew the drill: the coded message meant he'd be heading out of the country to go free someone. A hostage? A prisoner? Man, woman, child? No way of knowing until he was briefed. He understood time was crucial and he couldn't stop by the village and make explanations to Tina about why he was about to disappear into the night.

Accepting orders had been easier when he was tucked in the military net of Fort Bragg. A summons like this was expected there. Now?

He had to go. He knew that. But a part of him ached to stay right there in Kirkwood Lake, enjoying Thanksgiving with his family and Tina.

Maybe next year.

He swallowed a sigh and texted back: Love that album, especially While You Were Sleeping.

That meant he'd be on the red-eye as expected. He scribbled a note to his mother, and walked back out the door.

He longed to stay and be part of the festivities, to take his place at the table with everyone else. Share this first beautiful holiday with Tina, thanking God for so many blessings. His time with his father, his time with Tina.

He'd told her that Thanksgiving was tough on soldiers. He'd meant it. Leaving his childhood home right now was one of the hardest things he'd ever done, but he had no choice. Not yet, anyway.

They'd booked him a flight out of Erie. With clear roads he had just enough time to get there and board.

He got back in the car, headed south and grabbed I-86. And just like that, he was gone.

Chapter Ten

Giddy anticipation lightened Tina's step as she set three pies into the backseat of her car at noon on Thanksgiving. She'd baked fourteen pies in the restaurant kitchen, enough to get them through three busy days of customers. With the success of the park light display in full swing, the *Kirkwood Lady* decked out in brilliant splendor for her cruises around the lake and the influx of customers in the lighted village each evening, preparation was key. Helping Laura made her feel better, like the happy ending to a made-for-TV Christmas movie, where everything comes out all right in the end.

She carried two pies into the Campbell house, ready to celebrate a grand if subdued Thanksgiving with all the Campbell kids in town for the first time in several years. Charlie's illness made for a command performance, but at least they were all here.

She stepped into the kitchen and was immediately grabbed by Max's younger sister, Addie. "It's Thanksgiving for certain. Tina's here and we've got pie!"

"A bunch of them." Tina handed the first pie to Addie, the second one to Cass, Max's other sister, and gave each Campbell daughter a quick half hug. "Can you guys set these on the small sideboard, please? I've got to go grab the caramel Dutch apple from the car."

"I say we take a detour to the fork drawer, grab what we need and follow the sage advice of 'Life's short. Eat dessert first,'" joked Cass.

"I'm in." Addie pulled the pecan/sweet potato pie closer and breathed deep. "Reason enough right here to move back to Kirkwood and have Tina as a roomie. As long as you cook and bake like this we'd be the perfect match, because none of my mother's cooking skills rubbed off on me."

"I had a special request to make that one again." Tina waved toward the pie in Addie's hands as she moved back down the side stairs. "Seth talked it up, and I promised Max he could try it."

"But Max isn't here."

Tina stopped on the short stairway and turned. She shifted her attention from Addie to Cass and back again. "Not here?"

Cass shrugged Max's absence off, which meant Tina was doing a great job of hiding her disappointment. "He got called back."

"Called back?" That couldn't be right. Why would Max get called back into service? He was done, wasn't he? Or at least on leave because of his father's deteriorating condition until his official time was over.

"That's what we're assuming, anyway." Addie's expression said she wasn't all too sure of anything. "Mom said he left a note saying he'd get back as soon as he could and not to worry."

"Which means we probably should worry," added Cass, but then she made a face that said worry and Max went hand in hand. "But this is Max we're talking about, and he always goes his own way."

"And comes out of it with barely a scratch," Addie said as she moved toward the dining room. "Nice trick."

"Tina!" Jenny bustled into the great-smelling kitchen as the girls moved off to the dining room. "You brought the most delicious pies, thank you! Come in, dear, let me take your coat."

Tina hesitated, breathed deep and tried to smile. "I've got to go grab the apple pie. I'll be right back."

"Wonderful," Jenny went on. "I'd really hoped to have everyone here for the first time in years, but Max's call-up changed things. So now my hope is we can regather with all the family at Christmas as long as Max is done saving the world."

Saving the world.

Doing his job.

Tina swallowed the lump of disappointment that had taken up residence in her throat.

Max was gone. Without a word. Without a mention. Just...

Gone.

I'm here to stay, home for good, he'd told her.

Not true, obviously.

He'd lied.

Like so many others in the past, people who'd made promises they hadn't kept. Max had pulled out all the stops to tip her heart in silly, gleeful directions, then left.

She walked to the car feeling partially shell-shocked and habitually stupid. She'd suspected from the beginning, hadn't she? She'd held back from the get-go because she knew Max, and she should be experienced enough to avoid bad-ending entanglements.

She'd messed up, and she didn't want to go back inside and pretend everything was all right. She didn't want to put her game face on and go through a family-filled af-

ternoon that reminded her of how lame her family relationships were. She wanted to jump into the car and drive
hard and fast—with the pie, of course—grab a fork and eat
the whole thing with a pint of ice cream and watch stupid,
lame happily-ever-after movies while she cried.

Except that would make Charlie and Jenny sad.

She didn't do any such thing, because inside the quaint
lakeside Colonial was a family who loved her, minus one.
A family celebrating what might be their last Thanksgiving with Charlie. A family grounded in faith and love. No
matter that Max had done his typical "here today, gone
tomorrow" vanishing act while grabbing her heart in his
short stint home.

Her fault.

She'd watched him do the same thing from a distance
as a teen. She'd longed from afar then, but should have
learned her lesson over the years.

For whatever reason, choice, destiny, fate or Providence,
the movie-style happily-ever-after eluded her in matters
of the heart.

Serving coffee was different, Tina realized as she strode
back toward the house, determined to put on a good front.

With coffee, she knew the rules of a good brew, inside
out and backward, the friendliness of being the neighborhood barista without getting too close.

Baking? Her mother's artistry in the kitchen bred true.
Tina loved creating, finessing and developing great recipes, the kind that make people smile.

Family?

A chasm in her heart tore open again, a rent that should
have healed long ago, as she approached the side door.

Family eluded her. Romance crashed and burned around
her. She'd thought...

No, she'd hoped—

It would be different with Max. She'd fallen for him hard, and that was as much his fault as hers, because he'd led her on deliberately.

She drew a breath, blinked back tears, planted a smile on her face and walked back inside, determined. Today was Charlie's day. A Campbell holiday, through and through.

And she'd promised to help them through the busy holiday season, but come January?

Brockport or Spencerport, here I come.

Mrs. Thurgood hurried into the hardware store late the following week. "Tina, I had to see you! I've just gotten the lease for the apartment under yours, and I'm so excited to be your new neighbor!"

Tina couldn't deflate the joy on the elderly woman's face by saying she'd be leaving soon. Happiness shone in the widow's eyes, her smile, the very way she walked. She gave Mrs. Thurgood a big hug, then took a step back. "Now, what about moving day? Do you need help, because there are a bunch of us who would be glad to step in. Zach and Luke both have trucks, and Seth's SUV would hold a lot of stuff."

"That's the nice thing," the old woman explained. "The furniture is staying, and I don't think we need a truck for my clothes. I'm not bringing the bulk of my stuff with me. I figure next summer I'll head back to my place and go through everything, clearing things out, donating this, tossing that. It's easier to do when the weather's nice," she added, as if the reason she'd let things pile up was weather-related.

"Sounds good." Tina patted her hand, wishing things could be different, knowing it was impossible. "And I'm happy to come help."

"You're busy enough." Mrs. Thurgood leafed through

a few paint chip cards, her gaze sharp. "Mrs. Benson said I should pick out new paint for the living room. If I drop it off at the apartment, her son will paint the walls on his day off and we're good to go."

"Take them out on the step," Tina advised, pointing toward the front door. "The color is more true in natural light. But it's cold out there, so don't take too long to decide."

"I will! That's a right good idea, Tina Marie!" Mrs. Thurgood hurried outside as Sherrie came through the back door, holding a magazine high.

"This book is filled with great nursery ideas."

"Awesome." Tina turned a fake but bright smile her way.

Sherrie looked close, then moved in and looked closer yet. "What's wrong?"

"Nothing." Chin down, Tina accepted a set of wrenches from a customer and ran them through the scanner. "That will be $22.47, please."

"Nothing?" Sherrie made a face, waited until the customer had checked out, then stepped in front of Tina. "What do you mean nothing? Of course there's something wrong, I can always tell, that's why you can't possibly leave because we've got this, this…" She waved her hand back and forth between them. "Connection thing. And it's not right to mess with stuff like that, Tina."

"We do have a thing," Tina admitted, but then she made a face at Sherrie. "And I'm still leaving. I have to, Sher." She drew a deep breath and lifted her shoulders. "But not for a few weeks and we'll get the nursery done first."

Sherrie stared at her, then glanced around the hardware store. She paused, listened, then sighed. "Max is gone."

"I don't want to talk about this."

"When did he leave? And why?"

"He left on Thanksgiving, and I have no idea why. End

of conversation," she warned as Mrs. Thurgood bustled back through the front door.

"It is downright cold out there!" Mrs. Thurgood plunked the paint chips down and pointed. "Vanilla Latte Romance, right there. I think that would be lovely in a living room, don't you, Tina?"

Right now the word *romance* was enough to put Tina over the edge, so she moved to the paint mixer and pried open the can of pastel tint base.

"Of course, it's kind of plain, but I can spruce it up with some pictures, don't you think?"

"Pictures make the room," Sherrie agreed. She looked hard at Tina, but no way was Tina about to bare her soul in front of Mrs. Thurgood, or anyone else for that matter.

"Just one gallon, Mrs. Thurgood?"

"That's what the landlord said, so I'm following directions."

She smiled as she said the words, and when Tina walked the can of paint out to Mrs. Thurgood's car, a middle-aged woman carrying a bag from the local deli raised her brows in approval. "Aunt Elsie, let me put this back here." The woman took the can of paint from Tina and tucked it into the trunk. "We can drop it off at the apartment. You should be ready to move in within a week." She turned toward Tina. "I'm Elsie's niece, Rachel. She told me she needed to make some changes and I came to town to help her."

"Oh, goodie!" Mrs. Thurgood said the words with false enthusiasm, as if none of this was her doing, and yet…she had little choice but to do it.

Tina understood that too well, and was just as annoyed by the sudden turn-around in her own life.

Which is understandable at her age, her conscience berated. *At yours? Ridiculous.*

"It's nice to meet you." Tina stretched out a quick hand

to Mrs. Thurgood's niece. "And thanks for coming to town to help Mrs. T. She's a favorite around here."

"Family's important," Rachel replied. She tucked the grocery sack into the trunk and helped her aunt into the front seat. "Have a nice Christmas if I don't run into you again."

"You, too." Tina said the words, but the thought of nice Christmas seemed anathema, and that emotion shamed her. She had a lot to be grateful for, she knew that.

But she'd gotten all tied up and emotional over Max, and having him disappear from her life?

It hurt.

"We need a painting date." Sherrie greeted her as she came through the door, clearly determined.

"Right after Christmas," Tina promised. "Everything slows down that week, even though the park lights are still going then. The store will be quieter and I can sneak away for a day."

"Excellent!" Sherrie hugged her and left.

She placed a call to the Realtor once Sherrie had gone home. "Myra, it's Tina. I think I'd like to take a ride to see those Brockport and Spencerport locations fairly soon, but I don't think I can do it before Christmas. We're short-handed here at the hardware store, and—"

"No worries!" Myra's voice sounded like so many others, alive with Christmas cheer.

Blech.

"December is pretty much wasted when it comes to doing deals," Myra explained, "so you go ahead and have a merry Christmas—"

Tina had to hold herself back from explaining the unlikelihood of that possibility.

"And we'll see them in January. That way the hardware store is quieter and I'll have time to make the drive with you."

"You don't think the locations might rent or sell by then?"

Myra's calm offered reassurance. "Well, they could, but it's unlikely. And the way I see it is if it's meant to be, it will be."

"Que sera, sera."

"I love that old movie!" Myra's voice pitched up. "How did you hear about that at your age? It's ancient by today's standards."

"It was a favorite of my mother's," Tina replied. Saying the words made her remember her mother playing the classic movie, loving the suspense of the story, and the melodious tones as Doris Day sang the old lyrics. "She used it as my lullaby when I was little."

"I did the same thing," declared Myra. "The babies loved it, such a sweet song. But most don't know it now."

"I do."

"Call me after Christmas," Myra reiterated. "We'll plan a day in early January, unless things change between now and then."

"They won't. I can guarantee that." Tina said the words with all the finality they deserved.

Myra laughed. "Another thing I've learned over the years, Tina… You wanna hear God laugh? Tell Him your plans."

Meaning God was in charge, first, last and always.

Tina had a hard time with that scenario. It seemed each time she tried to let go and let God take charge, something went awry. In this instance, that something was the broken heart she'd been nursing since Max had disappeared a week ago.

No call. No word. No email, no text.

Nothing.

As if Max had fallen off the map completely.

His mother had taken it in stride. She was Jenny Campbell, a woman of faith and grace.

Tina?

She wanted to go a few rounds with a punching bag, and not one of those big, heavy body bags, no, sir. The light, hanging-high variety would do, and she'd pummel away at that thing until she wasn't mad or disappointed or sad anymore.

Ever.

She crossed the street near the end of the day and entered The Pelican's Nest through the kitchen door. Han brightened the moment she stepped inside. "It's like old times again! Three nights this week make me so happy!"

"Me, too." She pulled out a clean apron, and began setting plates for orders. "It feels good to be in here, working with you again."

"It feels right because it is right." Wisdom deepened the cook's lined face. "It was wrong to have you gone from this place. I like this better."

Ryan came through the short passage leading from the dining room to the kitchen. He spotted Tina, stopped short and stared, then spun on his heel and walked out.

Tina turned toward Han. "He hates me."

Han shrugged. "He doesn't know what he feels, I think. He spent too much time listening to his father, and all he heard was how you ruined their business, ruined their lives. And you did none of this," Han reassured her as he grated cheese over a fresh pan of lasagna. "But Rocco always needed to blame others. You were an easy target. Now, we can fix this."

He sounded so sure, so certain.

But could they fix things?

Laura came into the kitchen and gave Tina a spontaneous hug. "I'm so glad you're here tonight. I was just going to call you and see if you could come over. We just got a reservation for a senior citizens bus tour. They're coming to see the lights before they do some shopping in the village. Then they're gathering here for a late supper at seven forty-five. I don't think we could manage it without you, Tina."

"Then it's good I'm here."

Laura moved closer. "What's wrong? What's happened?"

"Ryan is rude to Tina and makes her feel bad." Han minced no words. "He needs to be polite to anyone who helps. All of the time."

"You're right," Laura admitted. "I'll talk to him."

"That might make it worse, Aunt Laura." Tina shifted her attention toward the door. "He's already an angry kid. He lost his father six months ago, he's working all the time and doesn't appear to like it—"

Laura acknowledged all that with a nod, but said, "That doesn't give him the right to be mouthy and rude, Tina."

"But that was the example he lived with for so long." Tina scrunched her face and shrugged. "I'm hoping that time will help heal him. That if he's around me, he'll see that I'm not a terrible person."

"This has not worked so far," Han reminded them. "And Tina has been here many days to help. Ryan should be polite to all."

"I agree." Laura turned back to Tina. "The days of our family treating each other poorly are over. And I'll see that my son understands that, Tina."

The back door slammed shut, which meant Ryan had been in the doorway, listening.

Laura's eyes darkened with worry. "When I see the anger in him, it reminds me of his father."

Tina couldn't disagree. "But he looks like my dad, Laura. And there wasn't a kinder, more generous man than Gino Martinelli."

Laura acknowledged that with a look outside toward the cemetery. "I go to their graves sometimes, Tina. To apologize. To beg forgiveness. But it's too late, of course, and they died hating me, thinking I was a terrible person."

"They were angry, yes, especially at first." Tina shrugged and shook her head. "They felt betrayed because they trusted you with the restaurant, with me, and when you let me go, Dad was too sick to do anything about it. So he was sad. But mostly they thought you married the wrong person, and that Rocco wasn't good for you. And I agree. But they never stopped loving you, Aunt Laura, and they did forgive you before they died. And the first thing my father would say if he heard you now?"

Laura lifted her chin, wondering.

"He'd say head over to that church and get right with God. Because He's the only one we ever need to please."

Laura swallowed hard. One hand gripped the other, tight. "I haven't gone to church in a long time."

"No time like the present to start." Tina smiled at her. "If you want, I can go to the early service, then come here on Sunday and you can go to the later one. That way the restaurant is covered and we both have church time. And then I'll work at the festival booths as scheduled."

"It's a very sensible plan," Han told Laura. "How blessed are we to have a church right across the street?"

Laura looked from one to the other. "I'd like to try that, but not this weekend with the festival craziness on top of everything else. Maybe next weekend, okay?"

It was a start. "Good." Tina nodded agreeably as she grabbed two new orders off the wheel. She handed them to Han as she prepped the plates, but she couldn't erase the anguish she'd seen in Ryan's gaze. He wasn't just angry, although that would be bad enough. He looked wretchedly sad, and seeing that look on her young cousin's face broke her heart. She didn't want her presence to deepen his sorrow, but Laura was right. Ryan needed to find some level of acceptance, and she hoped it would be soon.

The night proved to be as busy as Laura had expected and it was late by the time they closed things up. Tina walked home, missing Max, pretending not to, and half dreading the busy Main Street Festival weekend. She'd be up well before dawn, baking in the restaurant kitchen, getting a head start on a frenetic day. No major snowstorms were expected to mess with the festival, and that was a blessing right there.

She approached her door and sighed. She was surrounded by a Christmas village, lit up and sparkling against a thin layer of fresh, white snow, but her little apartment seemed bare.

She'd been running back and forth between the hardware store and the restaurant, barely stopping for breath, leaving no time to make her little apartment festive.

Because you don't feel festive, her conscience reminded her. *You're mad at yourself for falling for Max, you're mad at Max for leaving and you have no real clue what you want to do with your life. Can't we go back to the "let go and let God" idea? Because it was a good one.*

Life without a firm plan? Without a goal? Without a schedule of events?

The very thought made her antsy.

But then she paused with her key in the lock, turned and looked around.

What had all her perfect planning gotten her? An estranged family and a burned-out café.

Despite her devoted scheduling, life had turned the tables on her. Sherrie's face came to mind. So happy, so excited about the upcoming birth of her son. But she'd sat with Sherrie for long hours after her earlier miscarriages. She'd held her hand, taken long walks and prayed for Sherrie and Jim.

She hauled in a deep breath and scanned the old café site from her stoop.

Life didn't come with guarantees. Maybe, just maybe, she needed to let go more and plan less. She glanced at the clock tower, saw the time and hurried inside to catch some sleep, determined to adopt that mind-set more fully on Monday.

After the insanely busy Main Street Festival weekend.

Chapter Eleven

A tiny *ping* against Tina's window disturbed her sleep. She rolled over, glared at the clock, saw the middle-of-the-night hour and went back to sleep.

Ping! Ping! Ping!

Hail? Freezing rain? A sleet storm?

Her brain pictured and discounted each of those possibilities as she squeezed her eyes shut and thumped the pillow into a better position. The repeated noise came again, sounding like pellets, lobbed against her window. She pried one eye open and peered at the night sky through her front window.

Starlit with a waxing crescent moon.

There was no storm, and barely a cloud in the chill, December sky.

So what woke her? Groggy, she hauled back the covers and crept to the window. Beyond the short space of Overlook Drive, the town lay quiet and still. The main holiday lights of the town-wide Christmas festival went dark at midnight each day, but the arched streetlights of Main Street still glowed. The white twinkle lights robing the village trees brightened the long, winter night.

All is calm.

All is bright.

Until another rain of pings pulled her to the other window. Careful, she tipped the edge of the curtain swag back to glimpse what was going on.

Max Campbell stood on the sidewalk below, gazing up.

He pegged a few more tiny stones at the glass. She flinched, and that tiny movement gave her away.

"Tina!" He'd spotted her. His voice was a loud whisper, one she intended to ignore.

"Tina Marie…" His voice came again, not quite so softly. Did he know the apartment downstairs was empty, or did he not bother to worry that he might be waking innocent people from a badly needed night's sleep?

Like her.

"Tina, I'm trained at breaking and entering as needed, but I don't want to spend the next five years in jail. Come down and open the door. Please?" He added the last as an entreaty, and if he was trying to be funny, well…he failed. And go downstairs and open the door for him after his little disappearing act that broke her heart into a million Max Campbell-loving pieces?

That wasn't about to happen. Not in this lifetime. She closed the curtain, put in a pair of cheap but effective earplugs and went back to bed.

Morning would begin their two-day festival of fun, food and frolic. Vendors set up heated tents along Main Street, and the high school opened its doors for cottage-style shops. Homemade pies, breads, jams, scarves, woolens, candles and art… Craftsmen from all over Western New York, Ohio and parts of Canada gathered to sell their varied wares this second weekend before Christmas. In less than two hours she needed to have the restaurant ovens cranking out baked goods. Rainey McKinney was doing the same on the farm, and Lacey Barrett would supply apple fritters, fried apple pies and glazed cider fry cakes.

Knowing how crazy the weekend would be, and how busy her past two weeks had been, the last person she wanted to see right now was Max Campbell.

Untrue, untrue, untrue!

Tina hushed the internal chastisement and curled up under the covers, ready to ignore everything in favor of a few hours of sleep. Whatever Max had been doing, whatever his vitally important role in the world was, she didn't care.

So there.

"Tina."

She turned from the double oven in The Pelican's Nest kitchen when Max called her name the next morning. Her flat expression said she wasn't one bit happy to see him. "You're back."

Her cool tone said his rapid disappearance put them back at square one. He had no choice but to own this guilt. Procedure dictated that he had to follow orders and maintain radio silence, but now he was back, and this time? He was here to stay, even if it took a while to convince her of that.

"Yes." He moved forward, but she waved him back, away from her domain.

"In case you haven't noticed, the entire town is busy this morning because it's day one of our Main Street Festival weekend, so I have a lot to do. In ninety minutes, people will be streaming in from all over. We have shuttle busses coming from the south end of the lake every quarter-hour so we don't over-tax the parking up here. Your mother is running the hardware store—she could probably use a hand there, and as you can see, I'm swamped."

"Tina, I know you're angry with me," he started, but she pivoted sharply, shot him a look and shook her head.

"I'm not. I'm angry with me because I knew better, Max. And that's not your fault, it's mine. I should have left well enough alone. Blame it on sentiment, hormones, whatever you'd like, but I'm over it."

"Over us?" He took a small step closer, encroaching.

"There is no 'us,' Max."

"I disagree."

"Well." She slid one tray of old-fashioned sugared Christmas cakes out of the oven and slid another tray in, set the timer and turned. "It's not up for argument. I'm glad you're around to help your parents. They're definitely more relaxed when you're here, and that's good for both of them. Now if you don't mind—" she indicated the door with a cool glance "—I've got work to do."

The chill in her voice matched her remote expression. He wanted to stay and state his case, but a public forum during a crazy busy morning probably wasn't the best choice.

"I'll see you later, then. And Tina?" He waited until she turned his way once more, her face void of expression. "I didn't have a choice about staying or leaving or talking about my assignment. I couldn't tell you or anyone else what I was doing, and that's how my life's been for the past ten years." He raised his shoulders, hoping she'd under-stand. "But for the first time ever, I wanted to." He turned and strode out the door, letting it click softly behind him.

He walked across the street to the hardware store, went inside, punched a back room cutting block several times, then sighed.

Tina wasn't just angry.

She was tomboy spittin' mad, and that meant a bouquet of flowers wasn't going to fix this. He'd only done his job, and done it well, but having to disappear when he'd gained her trust betrayed her growing faith in him. Knowing her history, he understood.

But that didn't change the bad timing, and Max's track record didn't gain him any points.

He manned the first floor of the store for the day while most of the action was in the streets of the lakefront town. People milled about, some dressed in Dickensian costume, mobs of families, carolers, and a horse-drawn carriage ride that took people up and around the old cemetery and through the park before bringing them back down into town, ready to shop and eat.

This festival hadn't existed when he was young. The whole thing was new, busy, saturated with people and goods, and totally Christmas-themed. A huge red-and-green arrow pointed to the back door of the hardware store, emblazoned with the words Jenny's Country Cove. His mother had taken domain up there for the day, because her old-fashioned housewares store was the perfect go-to site for reasonably priced country and Americana-themed gifts. Streams of people came in throughout the day, taking the stairs to the second-story shopping space, buying bags of country-themed items. They'd broken sales records by midafternoon, and that level of business commanded respect.

No wonder Tina was run ragged.

It wasn't just that he was called away at a busy time. He'd left others holding the bag, leaving them to make good on his promises.

A town-wide family festival, a marvelous cooperative endeavor, and the person he most wanted to share it with wanted nothing to do with him.

Mrs. Thurgood stopped by the store an hour before closing time with a small sack of roasted nuts and a little bag of Tina's sugar cakes. "I brought you a treat," she exclaimed. She handed over both bags.

"I couldn't, Mrs. Thurgood," Max protested, but the old woman wasn't about to hear any such thing.

"You can and will," she insisted. "I wanted you to know how much I love the light display in the park. Butch would have loved it, too. He'd be so tickled to have his things out like that! At night, they light up so perfect that I don't think it could be better, Max. And that's what I wanted to talk to you about. You know I'm moving, don't you? This week, actually."

Max shook his head. "I wasn't aware."

"Oh, that's right, you've been gone." Her expression said that had slipped her mind. "Well, I'm moving into the place below Tina's. It's just freshly painted. I used Vanilla Latte Romance from right over there." She pointed to the paint chip display on the far wall. "And Tina's going to help me hang pictures to make it homey."

Of course she was, because Tina was about the nicest, most helpful person on the planet. Not that she realized that about herself.

But Max did. "It will be beautiful, Mrs. T."

"Thank you." She smiled up at him. "But here's the thing. I'd like to donate all those Christmas decorations to the town, if that's okay."

It took a few seconds for Max to get the gist of what she was saying. "All of them? Mrs. T., that's thousands of dollars' worth of decorations and lights. Are you sure you want to do this?"

"Absolutely certain!" Smiling, she reached up to pat his cheek. "You know, you remind me of Butch."

"I do?"

She nodded. "Tallish, broadish, kind of strong and square. My mother used to say he was 'barrel-chested'

and that was a good thing in a man. You know, Max..."
She looked off to the left for a few seconds, then drew her
gaze back to his. "I was real mad when I lost him. Real
mad. I was mad at God, at Butch, at the flag, at just about
everything that came around. And I could not get over it
for the life of me."

"But you did."

"Because your mama came and saw me regular. She'd
stop by and bring me a piece of cake or a slice of pie or
a dozen cookies, always saying she had this bit left over.
Now, no one in their right heads thought anyone raising
seven kids had a bite left over, but as she kept doing that,
I stopped being quite as angry."

"Time?" Max suggested.

Her expression said yes and no, but her words went further. "Prayer, more than anything. And those little visits,
Jenny Campbell stopping by to chat. She never minded the
clutter or the dust, she just sat down, happy as could be,
and let me talk until one day she grabbed my hand, gave
it a squeeze." Mrs. Thurgood wrapped her hand around
Max's and pressed lightly. "She said, 'Elsie Thurgood, if
any of my boys grow up to be half as tough, faithful and
courageous as your Butch was, I will consider myself a
success at motherhood.'"

That sounded exactly like his mother. Warm, affection-
ate and able to look beyond the chaos and the clutter of life.

"When I saw you come home, I knew," Mrs. Thurgood added.

"Knew...what, exactly?"

"That she was right," Mrs. Thurgood declared. "With
all the problems in the world, one good man *does* make a
difference, Max. A big difference. And I see that man in
you, just like your mother saw it in my Butch."

His heart melted.

He'd watched men die. He'd watched as they gave up their lives for their country, fallen in a new kind of war that broke all the rules.

He'd stood at funerals and weddings, he'd held the children and babies of fellow soldiers, but this old woman's words, going beyond the obvious and seeing the heart and soul of the soldier within?

That meant the world. He reached out and hugged her. "Thank you, Mrs. Thurgood. And I do believe I can eat a few of those cakes, after all."

"Well, our Tina made them, and they're worth every penny we pay for them. Such a treat each Christmas!" she exclaimed. "And now if only we could find a way to keep her here…" She slanted a bright look of interest his way.

Max half laughed, half groaned. "That will take some doing. She's not all that happy with me right now."

Mrs. Thurgood waved a hand that said Tina's anger was no big deal. Clearly she hadn't seen the steam puffing out of Tina Martinelli's ears that morning.

"She's been crazy busy for two weeks straight, and what that girl needs is some old-fashioned courting."

"I can't disagree, but in case you haven't noticed, we don't live in or near the courtship capital of the world, Mrs. T." Max swept the view of Main Street a quick glance.

"The *Kirkwood Lady* has their holiday dinner cruise going on," she replied. "And I just happen to have two tickets right here." She stuck two rectangular pieces of cardstock into his hand.

"My father said these were mighty hard to get." Max tipped a grin down to the older woman as he scanned the printed admissions. "How'd you score these tickets, ma'am?"

"That's for me to know," she sassed back, smiling. "One way or another, you talk our Tina into getting on that boat with you. Nothing like a peaceful dinner for two, surrounded by Christmas lights, to show a woman how you really feel."

"Thank you." He reached out and gathered her into another hug. "This is very nice of you."

She waved it off as if it was nothing, but Max knew better. In a small town like this, folks pretty much knew one another's financial status because they all shared the same nosy mail carrier. Mrs. Thurgood wasn't poor, but she had little put away for old age, and now she had to move out of a home that was already paid-off and into an apartment where she'd have to pay rent, utilities and medical bills?

Max was pretty sure she'd fallen on some tough times. Still, he knew better than to embarrass her. He tucked the tickets into his pocket as a small crowd of customers came down from upstairs while another group went up.

Ryan's obvious misery made Tina sad.

She'd waved it off with Laura, but the reality of the teen's frustration bit deep.

He avoided the kitchen when she was in it. He averted his eyes whenever he could. And when they did make eye contact, he was quick to drop his gaze.

She'd advised time, but his animosity weighed heavy on her shoulders. Why couldn't they be normal, like the Campbells? Why couldn't they shrug off drama from this day forward and get on with things?

She trudged home at the end of a long day, but when a group of carolers came out of the church parking lot, singing of angels and stars and newborn kings, her attitude softened. Mary and Joseph had faced multiple hardships. They'd done all right.

They believed. They took strength from their faith. Ryan's got no such basis.

She understood what a difference faith made. And while Laura seemed to think coming back to church was a good idea, Tina didn't fool herself that Ryan would willingly tag along. At least the uptick of business at the restaurant kept him too busy to run around with the little gang of troublemakers he'd befriended last summer, and that was a big plus.

She let herself into the apartment, climbed the steps and glanced around.

Her mother's favorite ornaments were carefully layered in big, plastic totes. Her prized collection of village pieces were wrapped and tucked away in similar fashion.

Every other year she'd pulled the totes out and spread the decorations around. This year she hadn't bothered.

Because you're having a pity party? Or because you're just too busy to think rationally?

The former, she decided. The thought shamed her. In a world where so many did without, she was blessed.

She'd unpack those totes tomorrow night, she decided. She'd fill her little place with light and love and laughter, a perfect ending to an amazing weekend. And not once would she think about Max Campbell, working half a block away at the hardware store.

She curled up on the bed and turned out the light, determined to keep Max out of sight and out of mind, but knowing he was back, and wanting to talk with her?

Made forgetting about Max an impossible task.

"Hey, Dad? Wanna take a ride in to check out the park lights with me?" Max wondered aloud a little after eight that night. His father had been at home alone all day, a surefire way to drive the older Campbell stir-crazy. "I want to make sure we don't have any blown bulbs or bad strings and it's easier with two of us."

"It's cold," Jenny warned from the kitchen, but the look she sent Max said she approved the invitation. "Make sure you guys have hats and gloves."

"I'm on it, Mom."

"I'll get my coat." Charlie lumbered from the living room chair, grabbed his thick shearling-lined coat and accepted the hat and gloves from Max with a smile. "Let's get this done."

"You and me."

Max drove into the village, stopped at the edge of the road's descent and sighed.

The town splayed out before him, glorious in the full spectacle of Christmas lights. Beyond the town, Park Road offered a spectacular backdrop of brilliant color. Festive lights ringed the lake, a circle of holiday splendor reflected in the waters below. And along the western shore, the *Kirkwood Lady* cruised quietly on its nightly holiday dinner cruise.

The effect of water, lights and color made for a stunning display.

"I've loved being a part of all this," noted Charlie softly.

Max fought a lump in his throat.

Was this the last time Charlie would see the beauty he helped create?

In God's hands.

Max knew that. He believed it. He understood the frailty of man. But he didn't have to like it.

"We can park up top and walk down the western slope," Charlie suggested. "That way we're not disturbing folks as they drive through the display."

They took the outer road around town, and Max did as Charlie suggested. From this higher vantage point, the lights played out from a new angle, but the only lights he noticed this time were two small squares on Overlook Drive.

Tina's windows, lit from within.

She'd had a long day, and he didn't dare approach her now. Tired and cross weren't the best conditions for heart-to-heart conversations. And her self-imposed timeline gave him a few weeks to wear her down, although it was easier when she was by his side in the hardware store.

She'd be helping there again, once the festival was over. And he'd spotted Tina's name on the church committee to distribute Christmas baskets to needy families the following week, so he'd boldly added his name to the list.

"We've got a bad string here," Charlie announced as they moved through the display.

Max noted the location in his phone.

"And you'll need to fix the reins on the reindeer," Charlie noted. "They're blinking on one side and not on the other."

"Will do."

Taking opposite sides of the narrow park road, they examined the lighting display, away from the stream of cars. Between them they noted two other spots in need of tweaking, but all in all, the lights looked great and they were three weeks into the display.

"Well done." Charlie high-fived Max as they reached the end, but then he took a seat on a tree stump and breathed in and out, not gasping for air, but none too comfortable, either.

"Dad." Max dropped low instantly, concerned. He took his father's hand and gazed into his face. "You okay? Should I get help?"

"Winded is all. Give me a minute. Not used to walking much these days."

Max prayed that's all it was, and when his father's

breathing eased, he nodded uphill. "I wouldn't object if you brought the car down here, though. Your mother keeps warning me not to overdo it, then I do exactly that." He slanted a grin to Max, a smile that alleviated some of Max's worry. "Mostly to get a rise out of her because otherwise she's way too bossy."

"I'll get the car."

"I'd appreciate it."

Max hurried up the outside of the lighted display, through the trees. The park show required one-way traffic. That meant Max had to bring the car around the long way. He worried each minute, thinking of his father, out of breath, sitting on a stump, alone at the bottom of the park slope.

When he finally swung into the small parking lot at the park's southern tip, his lights picked up a group of people, hovering around the spot where he'd left his dad a quarter hour before.

Adrenaline surged.

Max bounded from the car and raced up the short incline.

Zach Harrison turned and spotted him. "Hey, Max. It's nice you guys were able to make it over here tonight."

Zach's tone and expression said two things. First, that Max needed to calm down. Second, that everything was okay, and Max was overreacting.

He took a deep breath and walked up to the group, pretending nonchalance. "How we doin'?"

"Good!" The lights to their left brightened one side of Charlie's face, leaving the other side in shadow, but the visible side looked all right. And his breathing sounded normal. Charlie looked up at him, made a face and swept the gathered group a look of pained patience. "The minute someone says the word *cancer*, you can't breathe crooked without everyone sending up a panic flag." He softened his expression and smiled up at Max. "But I'm glad you went to get the car. These treatments might help slow the beast inside, but they slow me down, too." He stood and waved to the lighted park surrounding them. "We did okay, though. Right?"

"It's beautiful, Charlie." One of the guys from the town highway department grinned his approval.

"The best ever," added an unknown woman. "I think these old-fashioned displays really help focus on the spirit of Christmas, the reason we celebrate. I like that it's not a techno-show of lights anymore."

Charlie thumped Max on the back. "That's the kid's doings. When everything fell apart, our soldier got things back on track."

"Great job, Max!"

"Thanks, Max."

"Not bad." Zach fake-punched his arm, only it wasn't all that fake. "And remember, they're giving the trooper exam in February. You've got my vote, Max."

"I appreciate it. I think." Max made it a point to rub his arm. "But right now I'm going to focus on running Campbell's Hardware until Dad feels up to doing it himself. With no more side trips," he promised his father. His commander had made it clear that Max was officially off the books for the remaining few weeks of his current military contract. "You guys are stuck with me."

"Good." Charlie hugged him, and while Charlie had always been a hugger, this embrace felt different. As if he was ready to hand over the reins.

Max hugged him back. While the small crowd dispersed, he and Zach walked back toward the car with Charlie. "How'd you gather the crowd, Dad? Did you fake a heart attack? Call for help? I'm gone fifteen minutes and you managed to throw a party in the woods."

"My fault," Zach admitted. "I was doing a quiet patrol, saw him sitting there and pulled off. Before you know it, folks spotted us and wanted to pull out of line for the lights and talk to Charlie. I think we made Jake Menko's job hard tonight. He's on duty to keep things moving steady."

"Oops." Charlie pretended to look guilty, but failed. "It was kind of nice, seeing folks out here. I spent a lot of nights checking lights in years past. And Max, I mean it when I say this is the best display ever."

Max accepted that with grace. "I'll let Mrs. Thurgood know. She's pretty proud of her son's part in the whole thing."

"A deserving tribute." Charlie shook Zach's hand and climbed into his side of the car. "Thanks for hanging out with me, Zach. Kiss that baby boy for me, would you? And bring him around to see me."

"We will," Zach promised. "He's had a cold, and Piper is insisting we can't make you sick."

"She's right," added Max. "Dad might be ready to take more risks, but tell Piper thanks for being sensible."

"Oh, she's that all right." Zach grinned their way. "Focused, driven, sensible, bossy...and really cute."

"A town trait," Max muttered. He could take each of those words and apply them to Tina, and the fact that she was mad at him meant he needed to campaign in earnest. What better time than Christmas to win true love's heart?

He waved to Zach, backed the car around and exited the lower end of the park. As he passed Tina's place, her lights blinked off. Two dark windows stared out, mocking him.

Resolute, he hung a right and headed toward his parents' house. He had Tina's table and chair project to finish before Christmas. And once Tina was back to work on Monday, it would be harder to avoid him. In the meantime? He and his men had completed Operation: Mistletoe overseas, a mission that rescued two young women being held hostage by extremists in western Asia. The success of that endeavor said his skills at covert operations ranked high. Now?

He had every intention of launching a successful Operation: Tina much closer to home.

Chapter Twelve

"Tina! How are you doing?" Zach Harrison's sister Julia stopped into the sprawling festival food tent Sunday afternoon. Her two boys, Conner and Martin, gazed around the tent with hungry expressions.

"I'm good, Julia." Looking down, Tina focused on Zach's two little nephews. "And I have a Christmas cake with your name on it, Martin. You, too, Conner. If it's okay with Mom. Have you been good?"

"Very." Martin nodded with the seriousness of a six-year-old. "Conner was kind of a baby over at the ring-toss game because I got more rings on than he did, but then he said sorry." Martin's face said a simple apology didn't quite make up for pitching a hissy fit in public.

Tina fought a smile.

"Well, you took two of my rings, so that made me madder than mad." Conner glared at his older brother, and Tina had the distinct impression that before too long, Martin wouldn't be nipping anything from his younger brother, because Conner had almost caught him in size already, despite their two-year difference.

"Did not."

"Did so."

"Did—"

"Stop. Both of you. Or no cake. Got it?" Julia directed a no-nonsense expression their way, a look that said the boys better shape up.

They did.

"Here," she said as she handed over a deep box to Tina. "I was told to give this to you."

"Because?"

Lacey Barrett began to help the next customer in line, giving Tina a moment to step aside. She opened the box, stared inside, then turned, puzzled. "It's a crèche."

Julia nodded. "From the Holy Land."

"Olive wood." Tina grazed a finger across the burnished wooden surface, confused. "But who?" Tina hauled in a deep breath as realization hit. "Max."

"The man certainly has good taste," Julia noted as Lacey handed each of the boys a tree-shaped sugar cake. "I saw it on display at the high school, and then Max stepped up to the vendor, quiet and calm, plunked down a fistful of money and said, 'This is the kind of Nativity set a family hands down for generations.'"

A family hands down for generations.

Tina's heart pinched tight.

Family. Her small family, mending. Maybe?

His family, so strong, so loving, being torn by serious illness. And Max, sending her a beautiful, touching gift of Christmas, a hand-carved Nativity from the very land Jesus trod long ago.

"I think you like it." Julia smiled and Tina flushed.

"It's stunning. It's…" Words failed her.

"It's the kind of gift a man gives a woman he loves," Lacey noted once her customer left with a small box of apple fritters and two tins of cakes. "Looks like someone is staking a claim, Tina."

"Or has too much time and money on his hands," she replied, but the old-world glow of the polished wood called to her.

Was she being too stubborn, not letting him talk, unwilling to listen? Weren't these the traits that got her family into trouble? The long silences, holding grudges, stepping back?

A clutch of people came in, and business stayed steady the rest of the afternoon. By day's end, when the last of the baked goods had been sent to the homeless shelter in Clearwater, Tina was bone tired. The short walk home, carrying the box holding the beautiful carved Nativity, gave her a few minutes to think. To pray.

She was stubborn as a mule sometimes.

The gift in her hand reminded her of Mary's willingness to say yes to God. A young woman, asked to do the impossible, to carry the Son of God.

Mary said yes and changed history.

Let not your heart be troubled...

The promise in John's Gospel offered eternal life, but asked for belief. Was she careless in her belief? Did she voice it, but not live it?

Sometimes.

That thought troubled her, and as she moved up the walk, her gaze was drawn to her entrance into the house.

A thick fresh wreath decorated her door. Festooned with bright red ribbons, clusters of berries and white twigs, the wreath looked like Christmas and smelled like a fresh walk in a piney wood.

A card hung from the wreath, and Tina pulled it out, then stepped closer to the light. "It's always more fun to come home to a cheerful door. Merry Christmas, Tina. With love, Max."

She scanned the area, half hoping he'd be there.

He wasn't.

She placed her hand against the lush wreath, bright and welcoming, the velvet-soft scarlet bows nestled against spiny evergreen.

Traditions.

A traditional wreath.

A traditional Nativity.

Could he be wanting the very same thing she craved? A new normal with her? A chance to begin a new branch of the Campbells?

She went inside, climbed the steps and pulled out her phone, then hesitated when the screen flashed on.

She needed to be sure. Not about her own feelings. His disappearing act made her quite aware of how hard she'd fallen, how much she cared about Max Campbell.

What she needed more than anything was to be sure of *him*. And that required a little more thought and probably more prayer.

She reopened the crèche box, dusted a small side table and set up the beautifully glossed wooden Nativity.

Timeless and prayerful, the image of that first cold Christmas touched her heart. Mary had said yes to a contentious request, then Joseph vouched for her when he could have turned his back and walked away.

He hadn't. He'd trusted. He'd believed.

And that was something Tina needed to do more fully.

Max smoothed his palm over the finished patio tables, satisfied.

They'd been knocked around in the fire at Tina's cafe. Not burned, just singed, but smoke and water damage had joined forces against them. He'd dried them out, sanded them down and applied fresh summer-toned paint to each one.

He'd variegated the chair spindles, mixing and matching yellows, greens and blues, until the final cheerful effect saluted nice weather and waterside dining.

Would Tina love them?

He hoped so. More than that, he wanted her to have a piece of the business she'd worked so hard to build. Something tangible to show her investment of time and effort.

Four tables and sixteen chairs, a salute to her café. And to her. If she forgave him long enough for him to give them to her.

He glanced up at the clock, disappointed.

He'd hoped for a phone call tonight.

He knew Julia had presented Tina with the glossed wooden Nativity. He'd gotten her Mission accomplished! text late that afternoon while he'd finished the last of Tina's chairs.

And Tina would have discovered the wreath he'd fastened to her door a few hours ago.

Still no word.

Stubborn? Or wary?

Both, his brain reminded him. *With good reason. She's been hurt before and doesn't have a whole lot of reason to trust people lately. Take it slow.*

The reminder hit home, but the last thing Max wanted right now was slow. He craved the dream he saw before him, just out of reach.

Tina. A home. A family. A dog. Maybe two dogs.

He grinned as Beezer nudged open the door of the garage workroom. "Hey, old guy."

Beeze yawned, eyed the chairs, then yawned again.

"Time to head in?"

The dog's head bobbed in understanding, his tail beating a quick rhythm against the table leg.

Max led the way out, turned to shut off the light and gave the tables one last look.

Beautiful. Bright. Winsome. Like their owner. Now, if he could wear her down enough to bring joy back to those pretty gray eyes?

He'd be a happy man.

"When's Tina due in?" Earl asked Max shortly after noon.

In forty-two minutes and twenty-nine seconds.

Saying that would make him sound more desperate than a guy should ever admit to, so Max shrugged. "She's on the schedule for one o'clock."

"Then I'll wait and take my lunch once she gets here." Earl lifted a box of parts and carried it to the repair area in the back room. "I'll break down Dan Hollister's snow-blower in the meantime. Darn fool things cost an arm and a leg, then don't work when you need them most. I'm a plow man," he advised Max, and let the door swing shut behind him.

I'm a plow man.

Max grinned.

He'd been away from country-speak too long. Military conversations tended toward concise speech, rarely more than was needed. Right now he wanted time to pass quickly, counting the minutes until Tina walked through that door.

The store was atypically quiet. His mother had predicted that the rush of weekend shopping would give them a day or two of quiet time to recover, and Max busied himself with reorganizing the upstairs shelves. Displays had been jumbled over the hectic weekend, and his mother's life would be easier if she could walk upstairs with her little scan gun later that day and order new stock automatically. Her task would be simplified if everything was back in order.

"Max?"

Tina's voice, behind him. He turned slowly, tamping emotion when what he really wanted to do was grab her up, kiss her like crazy and set a wedding date for soon.

Very soon.

Stifling rampant emotions, he faced her. "I didn't hear you come in."

She shifted her gaze to the wide country stairs. "I just wanted you to know I'm downstairs. That way you can finish up whatever you need to do up here."

Polite. All business. Matter-of-fact. But he didn't miss the fact that she had actually come upstairs to deliver the message when she could have simply called out from below.

And that slight difference meant Tina Martinelli was maybe yearning—just a little—to see him.

The realization put him instantly in a brighter mind-set than he'd been minutes before.

He stepped forward, crowding her space. "Excellent."

She moved to go back down, but Max blocked her with an arm against the near wall. "That's it?"

"Yes." She gave him a look that said he might be wise to move his arm.

He had no intention of doing any such thing. "Really?" He edged closer, just close enough to see his breath ruffle her short hair. Close enough to watch her eyelashes flutter as she dipped her gaze. "Nothing else you want to say to me, Tina Marie?"

"Probably nothing that won't end up with me in jail. Men that take off for weeks without even the courtesy of a simple farewell or a note that says 'see you soon' don't deserve a lot of leeway when they finally show up again."

He acknowledged her words in a straightforward fashion. "The army's pretty tight on the 'need to know' rule.

They called me up on coded orders with radio silence. If I could have said goodbye, I would have. I promise."

She scowled, but her frown didn't look quite as intense as it had three days ago, and right now he'd take any hints of improvement he could get. "How about allowing me to make it up to you? I have tickets to the hottest gig in town and there's no one else I'd rather spend Saturday evening with than you, Tina."

"We have a hot gig in town?" Her arched brow said he must be thinking of another town because the terms "hot gig" and "Kirkwood" weren't exactly synonymous.

He grinned. "The *Kirkwood Lady*. Six-o'clock departure, a three-hour cruise with dinner, dancing and Christmas lights."

"How'd you get hold of those? They were sold out months ago."

"Well-connected." He hiked his brows to underscore his words.

He saw her weakening resolve when she lifted her eyes to his. "I have to help deliver Christmas baskets Saturday morning, then I'm working here in the afternoon."

"There may have been a slight schedule change," he replied. "I'm helping deliver the baskets, too, so Mom said she and Luke could take care of the store all day. That way you and I have a day off together."

"You rearranged my schedule for me?" She stood as tall as a five-foot-two woman could and glared up at him. "What makes you think you can do that, Max Campbell?"

He smiled. "Because my mother loves both of us and wants nothing more than to see us happy. If that means giving you some time off so I can court you properly, she was all for it."

"Max—"

"We don't have to hash everything out now." He stepped

back, giving her an out. She wasn't in a big hurry to take it, but then a customer came through the parking lot door, which meant Tina had to go back down. She started down, paused and glanced back up. Her over-the-shoulder look said he'd made up some serious ground, and that was something to be thankful for. "We've got time, Tina."

Max said they had time.

Did they? Tina wondered on Tuesday afternoon.

They did if she gave up the idea of investing her eventual insurance money somewhere else in January.

She pulled on her hat and gloves, tugged on her warm coat and walked through the park. The displays weren't nearly as eye-catching in the daylight. The combination of merry lights and darkness made them pop each evening, but strolling through them, seeing the work and time the men had put in, made her nostalgic for Kirkwood and she hadn't even left yet.

What is it you want?

She knew that answer straight off. To be happy.

What's stopping you?

Her first instinct was to list the bad things that had happened to her, but then she mentally grabbed a hold of her herself.

The only thing stopping her from grasping hold of happiness right now was her.

She turned and studied the village streets below. The snow had melted, and the dry pavement looked out of place for December, but the full parking lots, the sight of people moving here and there, a town alive with Christmas...

She loved that.

She raised her gaze to The Pelican's Nest.

She didn't just like working in her father's old kitchen. She loved it. She loved partnering with Han, the familiarity of old recipes, the connection to her parents, though they were now gone. But in their old restaurant, surrounded by childhood memories, she felt as if they were with her still.

She stared at the aging building.

It needed help, and Laura had no money. The whole place could use a good makeover, but Tina understood the downward dip of midwinter business. Laura was worried that she wouldn't be able to hang on until the busier spring season, and Tina agreed. It took a busy spring, summer and fall to make up for long, cold winters.

What if you combine forces?

The thought scared and elated her.

Would Laura think she was nuts? Would she even entertain such an idea?

Tina puffed out a breath. It frosted instantly, a tiny cloud of white, drifting upward.

May our prayers rise up like incense before You...

The frozen breath reminded her of that sweet, old prayer. Could she make this step forward? Should she?

God did not give us the spirit of timidity, but a spirit of power, of love and of self-discipline.

Timothy's verse hit home. Yes, she had a tendency to charge forward. Act first, regret later.

But this? Approaching her aunt about a partnership? This could be the full circle she'd yearned for. Faith. Family. Forgiveness.

She threaded her way through the park displays and headed toward the restaurant. It would be quiet now, a good time to catch Laura. She walked in, ready to present her idea, and found Laura in tears.

"What is it? What's wrong?" Tina crossed the few feet quickly. Laura snatched up the restaurant phone in one hand and shoved a piece of paper at Tina with the other. While she dialed 9-1-1, Tina scanned the brief note.

Mom, I've thought about this a lot and I know you'd be better off without me. I'm not a good person, not anymore. I'm sorry, Mom. So sorry. I love you, and I'll miss you, but this is the only choice I have left. I've been trying to get better, but nothing's working. Please forgive me, okay? —Ryan.

The chill of Ryan's words froze Tina's heart. She didn't wait to hear more.

There was only one person she knew who could figure out how to get to her young cousin and save him. And that was Max Campbell.

"Max!"

The desperation in Tina's voice brought Max running from the front of the hardware store. "What's happened? What's wrong? Is it Dad?"

She shook her head, eyes wet, a scrap of paper clutched in her left hand. "It's Ryan. He's going to kill himself, Max."

Mixed emotions climbed Max's spine. He scanned the paper, grabbed Tina's hand and raced across Main Street to the restaurant.

One look at Laura's face said she believed her son was capable of keeping his promise. "Laura, do you know where he might be?"

She shook her head.

"Has anyone checked the house?"

Again she shook her head, her voice struggling for words. "I was just there. I left Carly here to make salads for tonight—" she nodded toward the afternoon waitress "—and ran home for a few things. When I got back here, I found the note."

"You didn't see him, Carly?"

The middle-aged woman shook her head. "Not a peep. I'm sorry, maybe if I'd seen him—"

He'd gotten a forty-minute start. Where could a kid go in forty minutes? A kid who didn't drive?

Max's phone rang. He started to ignore it, but then he saw Luke's number. He answered quickly, staring at Laura while his brother spoke, then nodded, grim. "We'll be right there."

Fear claimed Laura's features. She reached forward and grasped his hands. "It's Ryan, isn't it? What's happened?"

"He's on the interstate bridge, threatening to jump, but Luke says he's hanging on for dear life and that's a good sign. Let's go."

They piled into Max's car. He drove quickly, following the curve of Lower Lake Road. The bridge came into sight once they rounded the point at Warrenton. A full contingent of lighted rescue vehicles said first responders were on-scene in full crisis mode.

"Max. Laura. Tina. Good." Zach Harrison moved forward, his expression taut. "He's scared, he's shaking and I think he's getting tired, which means his grip could slip."

"Let me talk to him," Laura insisted. "I think I can—"

"He wants you." Zach looked beyond Laura to Tina. "He says he needs to talk to his cousin Tina."

"Me?" The idea that Ryan wanted to talk to her during his crisis seemed ludicrous. The kid hated her. "Zach, I—"

"Tina. Please." Laura turned her way. "If he wants to talk to you, then please…"

"But—" Tina looked at Max. He met her gaze and shifted his to Ryan, standing on the bridge's narrow edge.

Max wanted her to do it. And she trusted him to understand a crisis situation. Crises were his forte, weren't they? *God, don't let me mess this up. I don't know what*

*to do or what to say, and I don't even know this boy. Help
me. Please. Give me words.*

She started forward, then a flash of inspiration hit. She
turned back. "I need you two with me."

Max's wince said that might not be a good idea, but Tina
stood still, adamant. "Laura is his mother, and Max, no one
is better skilled at emergency situations than you. Please."

The trooper commander hesitated, then nodded his
okay.

Max moved to Tina's right. Laura flanked her on the
left. Quietly, the three of them moved forward.

Strong emotion twisted the boy's face when he saw
them. He stared at his mother, then at Tina, and began
to cry.

Laura's face crumpled.

Max was just about to call a retreat when Tina took a
seat on the cold, hard bridge. "I'm here, Ryan. Ready to
talk. But it's wicked cold, there's sleet in the forecast, and
I'm scared that you can't hang on much longer, so do me
a huge favor, okay? Climb back to this side. Have a seat.
And we'll talk about whatever is going on, but I need you
to be safely on this side of the bridge or I honestly won't
have a clue what's being said, because I'll be worried to
death about losing my only cousin. I have two relatives
left, kid. You and your mother. I'd like to grow old with
both of you, if you don't mind."

His eyes widened as her words registered.

He stared at her, then his mother, then Max.

Max appraised the situation. He wasn't close enough
to make a grab for Ryan, and Tina's action would spawn
some sort of reaction. But would it be the reaction they
wanted? Needed?

*God, I know You're there, I know You're with us, and
right now, I could use some of that spiritual common sense*

*I'm usually so proud of. Because here, at this moment, with
the approaching storm pumping up waves on the lake?*

I'm scared.

Ryan gulped. His fingers moved. He studied each hand,
contemplating his choices. Moving slowly, Max and Laura
lowered themselves to the ice-cold bridge deck and faced
him, waiting.

"It's your turn." Tina met the boy's gaze and didn't
mince words. "Climb on over here and let's talk. Are you
okay to climb back over, Ryan? Because if your hands are
cold and you need help, we'll help you."

Max decided then and there that if he ever had a need
for a negotiating team in his future, Tina would be on it.
Her eyes, affect and tone stayed calm and neutral, offering the kid the lifeline he needed.

Ryan stared at her, gripped the rail tighter, then pushed
up. One leg came over. At the top of the rail, he faltered,
and for a long series of seconds, he looked like he might
fall, but then he pushed down hard against the railing and
brought his second foot up and over.

Max's heart soared.

This tiny leap of faith said Ryan didn't really want to
die. What did the boy want?

Max had no idea.

"Thank you." Tina nodded toward the bridge deck. "It's
cold, but it's the best I've got, kid. So what's going on?
What's got you this upset that you're thinking about throwing away God's most precious gift? Because frankly, Ryan,
that would break my heart."

"You."

Tina's steadfast expression faltered, but not for long.
"Because I've been helping your mom?"

He stared at her. Guilt and anguish fought for his features as he faced Tina straight on. Max looked from him

to Tina and back, then spoke softly. "Did you burn Tina's café down, Ryan?"

Ryan's face shadowed deeper. Tears streamed down his cheeks. His mouth crumpled and his jaw went slack. "I was with the guys who did it." He leaned forward after the admission, crying, his narrow back shaking with cold and remorse. "I didn't mean for them to burn it down, I thought they were just messing around. I knew Mom was running out of money and I thought—" He choked back a sob, then swiped a damp glove across his face. "I thought everything that happened was Tina's fault."

"Oh, Ryan." Laura's face reflected Ryan's anguish. "Honey, I—"

"Don't tell me it's okay." Ryan's voice rasped harshly. "I could have done something. I could have called the fire department, I could have tried to put it out, I could have…" He drew a deep breath and sighed, then shifted his attention back to the water. "Done something. But I didn't. I ran home, went to bed and acted surprised the next day. And then Tina turns out to be a real nice person and I ruined her life."

Tina started to speak, but Max held up a hand. "May I?" She nodded. "Please."

He faced Ryan more fully. "My best friend died when I was eighteen."

Ryan met his eyes, listening.

"I was with him that afternoon. He'd been drinking. Acting stupid. I knew he was drunk, I knew his girlfriend had been drinking and I was mad that they were being so foolish. I got disgusted and left." He hauled in a breath and shrugged. "It made me so mad that years of friendship were being washed away by a bottle of vodka, and I stormed off. I could have called his mother. I could have told his father." He shook his head. "I didn't. I went home, went to bed and the next morning I found out my buddy Pete and his girlfriend had been killed in a boating accident while I was sleeping. For nearly fifteen years I've carried that weight with me, Ryan. Wishing I'd called someone, alerted someone. Wishing I'd made better choices, but you know what?"

Ryan kept his eyes locked on Max. "What?"

"Here's the amazing thing about life. We generally get a second chance. And if we make the most of that opportunity and learn from it, we can turn the bad into good. But—" he directed a look toward the roiling water slapping against the cold, gray bridge "—not if we're dead, kid. Yeah, you shouldn't have spouted off about Tina, and you could have made better choices along the way, but when I went to see Pete's parents they reminded me of something. They said kids make mistakes because they're kids and that God understands kids better than anyone else. He knows they're a work in progress."

Reality broadsided Tina as she listened to Max's story.

Ryan and his gang had burned down her café. He and his buddies deliberately set a fire to destroy her business in an attempt to destroy her, to make her leave Kirkwood Lake.

Anger and regret vied for attention. Her hands clenched, envisioning the group of miscreants, torching ten years of hard work and dedication.

But Ryan's look of abject sorrow pushed her beyond outright anger.

He'd lived in a house surrounded by mistruths and slander. He'd been raised to think she was the enemy. And in a way, an in-your-face move like putting her coffee shop in the shadow of The Pelican's Nest made her the enemy.

She reached out a hand to Ryan.

He stared at it, then her.

"Ryan, we can't change the past. But together?" She swept his mother a look then returned her attention to Ryan. "We can run a wonderful business. But a family business should be run by family, kid. And more than anything else, once we get things squared away, I want you in. You. Me. Your mother, running the restaurant the way it should be run. What do you think?"

Laura held her breath while Max watched quietly. Ryan stared at Tina, then his mother. Disbelief shadowed his face, but then he started to creep forward, the cold, slippery bridge and his chilled limbs fighting the action. He made it over to them, and then clasped Tina's hand, tears still streaming down his young cheeks. "I think yes."

She clutched his hand, then pulled him in for a hug that Laura shared.

Max cleared his throat. "Why don't we head back? It's cold out here, and we've got a lot of good people who probably want to go home. Or at least climb back into their warm cruisers."

"You're smarter than you look, Max." Zach smiled at Max as he and Luke approached them. He led Laura and Ryan to a waiting ambulance that took Ryan to Clearwater Hospital for a mental health evaluation.

Tina and Max followed in Max's car.

Deep compassion for Max filled Tina, heart and soul.

Ryan's jaw had softened as he listened to Max's story. Max's confession had turned the boy's expression from grief-stricken to almost hopeful.

She looked at Max, really looked at him, and realized she'd judged him unfairly for years.

He'd shouldered unnecessary guilt a long time. How tough it must have been, living beneath a self-imposed cloud, wearing a mantle of blame. No wonder he avoided the Sawyers and stayed away.

Coming back must have been torturous, but Max did it because he knew his parents needed him. Their need trumped his badly placed guilt.

Her heart stretched wider, watching him.

She'd misjudged him. She'd taken what she saw as a kid and mushroomed it into undeserved resentment. And in spite of that he'd been nothing but kind to her. Gracious. Caring.

Loving?

Regret speared her because she'd cut him down pretty thoroughly since he returned from his final mission. And a man like Max, brave, daring, charismatic and caring, deserved someone who didn't make rash assumptions. Someone who could stand up to the test of time, not turn tail and run.

Seeing him here, in action, baring his heart to save a young man's life, she felt pretty undeserving of the brave and true soldier to her right.

But—

If given the chance again?

A tiny spark of warmth inside allayed the bitter cold metal beneath her, because if Max was willing to give her one more chance at that gold ring of love?

She'd never be foolish about taking it for granted again.

Chapter Thirteen

"Well." Max shoved his hands into his pockets while they waited for Laura in the hospital lobby. Ryan would have to pass a short series of psychological tests to prove he wasn't a threat to himself or others, but then he'd be free to come home.

Tina looked up at Max and patted the seat beside her. "You could sit."

"Sitting makes me antsy."

"And yet you sat on that bridge today, looking like you weren't freezing from the ground up and like you had all the time in the world."

"Just following a good example." He slanted a smile down to her.

"I was scared to death," she admitted. She reached up and shoved her hair back behind her ears. "My knees were knocking, my hands were shaking and all I could think was that the minute I opened my mouth, he'd know I was more afraid than he was. Only, you know what?"

Max raised one beautiful, thick, dark brow.

"All the fear disappeared the minute I started to talk to him. It was like God heard my fear and dissolved it.

I felt…" She groped for words, then shrugged. "Like a peaceful blanket got laid on my shoulders. Weird, right?"

"Not weird. God."

God.

Calming her. Helping her. Laying peace on her heart.

A rising trust swelled within her. Trust in God, in His path, in His timing.

"You were amazing out there, Tina. When you sat down and challenged him, I wasn't sure what he was going to do, but you made all the right moves. I was so proud of you."

Her heart melted at his words, his expression. "Max, I didn't know that stuff about you and Pete that day. I knew you were there, but no one ever let on that Pete and Amy were drinking. And I thought you were a jerk for never coming around again."

He shrugged like it was no big deal, but Tina read his eyes. She stood, crossed the small space between them and reached up to kiss his cheek. "I'm sorry I doubted you. And I'm sorry you carried that guilt around for all those years. It broke my heart to hear you talk about it."

He sighed, staring off, then shifted his attention back to her. "It's taken me a long time to face what happened that day. I've avoided coming home, I've avoided the water, I've avoided my family, all because I let guilt eat me alive. It was stupid." He waved off Tina's protest with an easy hand. "Hey, it's better now, so I can admit it was stupid to let it go so long, and that's why I'm so glad Ryan came clean. Because guilt makes for a real lonely partner in life."

Laura's approach halted their conversation. She reached out and hugged Tina, then Max. She wasn't crying. In fact, she looked strong, able and energized, more so than Tina had ever seen in the past. "I think he's going to be fine."

"Yes?"

She nodded to Tina, then motioned both of them to sit.

They did. Laura leaned forward and clasped Tina's hands. "I need to apologize to you."

"Laura, I—"

Laura gripped her hands tighter. "Let me say this. I know you and I have made progress, but Tina, our actions, mine and Rocco's, messed up more than our business. They messed up our son and ruined your café. Forgive me, please. Forgive us. And when you do that?" She offered Tina a small smile of entreaty. "I have a huge favor to ask of you."

Faith. Family. Forgiveness. Tina squeezed her aunt's hands. "Yes, I forgive you, and I'd like you to do the same for me. Resentment and revenge aren't good examples, either. Now, go for it. Tell me what you need, because that's what family is for."

"Take over the restaurant so I can take care of my son."

It took Tina several seconds to register Laura's request. "Laura, I—"

"Ryan's going to need some time, some therapy, and he needs to have a hands-on parent. More than he's had the past several years because, even before his father died, we were too busy working to do right by our son. On that bridge today I prayed, Tina. I prayed for the first time in a long time, and I told God I'd make better decisions if He gave me a second chance."

"And he did." Tina squeezed her hands lightly, understanding.

"Yes. So I know it's a lot to ask, and you probably think I'm crazy."

"First, you're not crazy at all, and I can totally see the Holy Spirit at work in this whole thing and I'm never going to question His timing or methods again."

"Huh?" Laura looked from her to Max and back.

"I was coming to the restaurant this afternoon to see if you'd like to become partners."

Laura's jaw dropped open. "You were?"

Tina nodded. "I'd been praying about my choices, and I realized that I'm happiest here, in Kirkwood Lake, working in a kitchen. So why not do it in your kitchen? The place where I grew up?"

"Are you serious?"

Tina sent a teasing glance to Max before bringing her attention back to Laura. "I'm generally way too serious, it seems, but in this instance, serious is good. So what do you think? We could partner up, you get more time off, and we build a café corner on the west end of the restaurant with my insurance money?"

Laura gripped her hands. "The best of both worlds."

"For both of us."

"Oh, Tina." She grabbed Tina in a big hug, a hug that said home and family and forgiveness rolled into one beautiful embrace. "This is perfect. I'll have time with Ryan and an income."

"And I don't have to move." She tipped a quick look toward Max, wondering what he thought of all this. Would he be delighted to have her in Kirkwood or had she totally ruined the beautiful chance at love he offered?

He stood. "Laura, are you staying at the hospital?"

She nodded. "Yes. Until they release him. I want him to know that I'll be by his side as long as he needs me."

He faced Tina more directly. "Then we better get going, because you have a restaurant to open in the morning."

Tina gave Laura one last hug. "Don't worry about anything and keep your cell phone charged in case I have questions. We'll have a lawyer draw up the legal stuff after Christmas, so for now, just relax and take care of Ryan."

"I will. And Tina? Max?"

They turned as they headed for the door.

"I don't know how to thank you enough."

Max met her gaze. "Right back at ya. Good night, Laura."

A crazy but fun week, Tina decided as the dinner rush wound down on Friday evening.

Max and Earl had pretty much taken over at the hardware store, Seth's daughter Tori was going to help there on weekends, and Tina and Han had been running The Pelican's Nest for several days. She'd planned menus, logged orders and checked food quality as vendors made deliveries to the kitchen door, loving every minute. The best part?

She felt like she'd come home after a long time gone.

She hooked the clean pots into place as Ryan walked into the kitchen. "Tina?"

She turned, surprised, because she hadn't seen him since they'd released him from the mental health evaluations a few days before. "Hey."

He came forward, a little nervous, but not stricken, and that was a huge improvement. "You look better."

He rolled his eyes as if that was an understatement. "I feel better. A lot better. Would it be all right with you if I came back to work?"

"Oh, my gosh, yes!" She grabbed his hands. "Yes, please! I missed you like crazy tonight, we were slammed from five o'clock on. It was downright insane for a couple of hours."

"You don't mind me being here?"

This time she stepped over the personal boundary lines and hugged her cousin for the second time since he was a preschooler, riding his Big Wheel up and down the driveway of his house. "I will absolutely love having you here. Family business means just that, Ryan. Family."

Laura stepped in behind him. She smiled at Han behind Tina, then clasped Ryan's shoulder. "We were just discussing that, and how we want this place to be like it used to be. The kind of spot that welcomes travelers and boaters and locals. Where everyone feels at home."

Her words reflected Tina's memories. Her parents had forged a delightful business just that way, by welcoming all who came through their doors. "When can we sit down and write up a schedule?"

"Monday," Laura answered. "I know you've got things going on tomorrow, so Ryan and I are going to work with Han and the girls to cover things, and then we'll go to the later service on Sunday if you can come over here after the early service and relieve us."

Laura and Ryan, going to church. Spending time together, rekindling faith. Planning with her as they reconstructed a Martinelli family business. Joy soared inside her. "That would be great. You sure you don't need me tomorrow?"

Laura smiled and shook her head. "Last I heard you were helping at the church—"

"In the morning," Tina countered.

"And then tomorrow night you have a date," Laura finished. "Max wanted to make sure things were covered here so you couldn't cancel on him."

"He said that?"

Laura grinned as she turned to go. "I believe his exact words were 'It took me weeks to get her to actually accept a date with me. Let's not give her a window of opportunity to wiggle out of it.'"

That sounded exactly like Max. Quick, funny and blatantly honest.

She turned the key in the lock a few minutes later, waved goodbye to Han and turned back to Laura and Ryan.

"I'll see you guys Sunday morning. And thank you both for making tomorrow night possible."

Ryan waved it off as if it was no big deal, but Laura grabbed Tina in a big, motherly hug, then stepped back and cradled Tina's cheeks in her hands. "Have fun, okay?"

A day off. A day with Max. A day to help others with Christmas and then relax as the *Kirkwood Lady* trolled the lake's perimeter, listening to Christmas music and eating fine food.

Her heart did a silly skip-jump in her chest as she returned Laura's hug. "I will."

"On the eighth day of Christmas, my true love gave to me..." Max intoned the old carol as they delivered the last boxes and baskets for the day. He climbed into the front seat of the church van and kept right on singing.

"You're really starting to get into this small-town Christmas stuff," Tina teased. "I expect this Christmas is quite different from last year's holiday."

Max considered that as he turned up Lower Lake Road. "Last year I was stashed in a Middle Eastern bunker, pretending to negotiate the release of accused political prisoners who were actually bargaining chips on a badly skewed administrative gaming table."

"Did the negotiations work?"

Max sent her a "what do you think?" kind of look. "They rarely do."

"Max." She leaned closer, almost kissably close, and laid her hand on his arm. "I'm sorry."

He shook his head. "Don't be. We got them out. Over the years I've learned that negotiating with terrorists generally falls under the 'no positive outcome' scenario. So we learned to go in and spring folks on our own."

"You rescued them?"

He nodded. "Safe and sound. One of them got married six months later and last I heard they're expecting their first child, a daughter, in about four months."

"Max." Tina tightened her grip on his arm. "That's wonderful."

He shrugged off the praise. "Just doing my job, Tina." He got out and walked her to her door, even though she argued that he shouldn't. "I'll see you tonight. I'll be here for you about quarter to six, okay?"

"Yes."

He looked down at her and let the intensity of his gaze wish for a kiss, but then he smiled, winked, stepped back and moved to the car.

It took every bit of willpower she had to not run after him and demand a kiss. The only thing that held her back was sheer and total embarrassment.

But the thought of kissing Max, of having an evening with him in a romantic setting, put her pulse in high gear.

The hours dragged on forever.

She tried reading, then ended up throwing the book across the room. She turned on the TV, knowing there was a weekend-long Christmas movie marathon on her favorite inspirational station, but seeing the happy glow on the heroine's face made the afternoon seem way too long.

She dressed with care and was ready impossibly early. That way she had plenty of time to wonder if her sour attitude had ruined whatever chance she and Max had.

He's taking you on a cruise tonight, her inner voice scoffed. *I think he's making all the right "I'm still interested" moves.*

She wanted to believe that, but did her overreaction mess things up? Then and there she decided that if Max was still interested…and she prayed he was…she'd work harder to be the best partner he could find, a loving and committed wife.

The doorbell rang.

Max.

She stood, slipped on her coat, scarf and gloves and moved to the stairs. The boat would be warm, but the walk over? Another thing entirely. She went down the steps, opened the door and paused, then sighed. Max stood in full dress uniform, looking way too handsome, strong and commanding. "You clean up nice." She tried to keep her words casual but he read the expression on her face and grinned.

"When a guy's working overtime to impress a pretty girl, he's got to pull out all the stops."

"About that?" She turned once she pulled the door shut behind her and faced him square, ignoring the chill breeze off the water. "I'm impressed enough, Max. Just the way you are."

His smile deepened, and he leaned in, brushed a too-light kiss to her mouth and held out his arm. "That's good to hear, but for tonight, you still get the full deal. Mrs. Thurgood assured me that's the best way to a girl's heart."

Mrs. Thurgood.

Tina smiled. With Jenny Campbell and Elsie Thurgood tweaking things, there was little room for failure. Walking to the dock with Max, Tina clung to his hand. The glorious lights of the village and town spread out before her, then ringed the lake like a circle of hope. A stream of traffic to their right aimed for the lighted park display, while tourists from all over the area milled the streets, snapping pictures and frequenting local businesses.

Drawn to the light.

The duality inspired her. From now on she would grab hold of the bright things in life: faith, hope, love and charity. With so much to be grateful for, old shadows would be banished forever, just like they should be.

She preceded Max onto the boat, and felt a rush of pride when folks greeted them as if seeing them as a couple was a wonderful thing.

"This way, please." The dinner hostess directed them to a linen-draped table. Tiny electric tea lights brightened each Christmas-themed centerpiece. Sparkling twinkle lights outlined the boat's frame, making it a traveling decoration during festival evenings. Bad weather had kept the boat moored a few nights back, but tonight the air was clear, if cold, and stars shone above with no snow predicted.

Tina sat down, smiled at the Gundrys across the way, then stopped, amazed, when Max Campbell dropped to one knee before her.

The entire cabin hushed, straining to hear. Tina was pretty sure that the loud beat of her heart would make that impossible. The sight of Max before her, gazing into her eyes and holding her hand?

Breath-stealing.

He grinned.

And suddenly warmth and longing nudged nervous and excited to the side. This was Max…

Her Max…

About to declare his love.

Or so she hoped.

He gripped her hand tighter. "Tina Martinelli, I know I'm making a spectacle of myself right now."

The other diners in the small cabin restaurant laughed and clapped.

"And I know you don't normally like to claim the spotlight, but on this occasion, I wanted everyone to know exactly what I was doing. And what I want. And that's to have you as my wife, Tina Marie." He paused long enough to let the words sink in. "To marry me. Grow old with me. Have some cute kids." He leaned in as if sharing a secret. "I do believe we've already discussed how many, but as I said then, I'm open to negotiations."

Tina couldn't help but laugh, and the rest of the boat laughed with her.

And then Max turned serious. Beautifully and romantically serious. "I love you, Tina. I didn't realize how much until I was called away last month, and if I had any doubts about a change of career, leaving here—leaving you—was the hardest thing I've ever done. So if you don't mind marrying an ex-army officer—" he withdrew a small box and flipped the top open "—I'd be honored to be your husband, right here in Kirkwood Lake."

Her heart lodged somewhere firmly in her throat, forming a lump so tight she couldn't force a word around it. Not long ago she'd watched as her hopes, dreams and aspirations burned to the ground, certain that her time in Kirkwood was over. For weeks she'd allowed the dark thoughts to cling tight, but in God's own amazing way…

In that perfect timing Reverend Smith liked to talk about…

Her life had changed and new dreams awaited her.

She reached out, hugged Max, nodded and fought tears. And then she kissed him, right there in front of a boatload of people, applause and shouts ringing in the moment.

"Is that a yes?" he whispered in her ear, his breath tickling her cheek, her neck.

"It is a total, unequivocal yes!" she whispered back, and when he kissed her again, she thought of a lifetime of Max's warmth, his strength, his faith and his humor—

And knew God had things under control.

Epilogue

"Hey. How's she doing?" Max tiptoed into the pink-and-green nursery the following Christmas Eve. "She seemed sniffly when I left this morning."

"Oh, she's fine," Jenny told him. She lifted the baby to her shoulder and snuggled her close. "Babies get sniffly for no good reason just because everything about them is miniaturized."

"Hard to believe it's been a year since I came back," Max whispered. "So much has happened…"

His mother's eyes filled instantly, remembering. "The way of life, isn't it? The good Lord gives and He takes away."

Max sank onto the window seat beside the glider rocker. "I'm glad Dad got to meet her."

Jenny's nod said she agreed wholeheartedly. "He was thrilled to have a namesake."

Mixed emotions tightened Max's throat. "Charlotte Grace Campbell."

"Charlie." His mother smiled up at him through her tears. "And if your dad saw what you did with this year's light show, he'd be pleased as punch, Max."

"You learned from the best," Tina said as she crept

into the room, bent and kissed Jenny's cheek, then did the same to Charlie's. "And as she grows up, we'll fill her with stories and pictures and beautiful memories of the grandfather that made all of this possible. And how God's timing worked so perfectly, bringing you home." She smiled up at Max and touched a finger to his cheek. "Bringing us together…"

"I think his patience might have been tried just a little on that part," Max drawled, meeting his wife's gaze.

She blushed. "Okay, that was all me, but then bringing Charlie just in time to meet her grandpa." She smiled up at Jenny and didn't try to hide the tears in her eyes. "That meant the world to me. To see him hold her. Talk to her. I might have been stubborn about going my own way before—"

Max cleared his throat to show he wasn't about to disagree.

She acknowledged that with a slight grimace of guilt, then added, "But for the first time in my life I saw God's hand in all of this. Giving me the family I always longed for, bringing me Max and Charlie, even in losing big Charlie." She raised her shoulders and touched the baby's soft-as-silk cheek. "As hard as that is, somehow it seemed like we'd all be okay because God gave us one another as He called Dad home."

Max's heart went tight, then soft.

They'd lost so much when they said their final goodbyes to Charlie, but when he looked around this room…

His daughter's bedroom, with his mother holding her ninth grandchild and the nighttime candle glowing in the window…

He saw Tina's words come alive.

God had given and God had taken away, but he was

blessed with so much more this year. A home, a family, a new life in Kirkwood Lake…

And a series of tomorrows, blessed by God.

He bent and kissed his mother's cheek, then his wife's, before he went downstairs to heat up the famous Martinelli red sauce. Thirty years ago he'd been a dirt-streaked kid dumped on Social Services four days before Christmas.

Now?

He was part of one of the best families on earth and despite life's ups and downs, Max Campbell couldn't be happier.

* * * * *

Dear Reader,

I love this story.

I love the reality of life forging on despite loss, the poignancy of Max's old guilt and Tina's genuine frustration as she works so hard to get all her ducks in a row...and then something messes with her well-thought-out game plan.

Forgiveness and guilt are the themes of this story. Max shouldered undeserved guilt as a kid and hasn't let it go in over a decade. How sad is that, and yet, I know many adults who carry a similar weight. He had to face his past finally in order to help his parents. Would he have shouldered that guilt forever if Charlie hadn't gotten sick? Who knows?

Tina fell between the cracks of family crises, her father's health and her uncle's tight-fisted, empty promises. Throw a couple of broken hearts into the mix and she's ready to kiss the whole thing goodbye and start anew.

But God's timing wins out, and I'm a firm believer in that. I remember a sports commercial with the theme "Be ready." An athlete spoke of how he trained hard, so that if he got called off the bench, he'd be ready with his A game. And when he was called to take the place of an injured teammate, he was at his best. God tells us that, too. He sent John to ready the way... He reminds us that we don't know the day or the hour, and to be ready when called.

With another joyous—and maybe poignant?—Christmas season upon us, I want to thank you so much for buying *Her Holiday Family*. From my family to yours, let me wish you a merry and blessedly peaceful Christmas, a time of joy and remembrance. God bless you!

And if you'd like to chat, I welcome the opportunity. You can snail-mail me c/o Love Inspired Books, 233 Broadway, Suite 1001, New York, NY 10279 or email me at ruthy@ruthloganherne.com. Come visit my website at ruthloganherne.com, cook with me at www.yankeebellecafe.blogspot.com and/or find me on Facebook! And feel free to stop by Seekerville, our delightful multi-author blog at www.seekerville.blogspot.com. The coffee's always on, and I'll make up a stash of cookies, just for us!

With cheerful blessings!

Ruthy

Questions for Discussion

1. Tina has worked at becoming a loner. Two failed romances, a singular business, family rejection and loss of her parents has left her guarded and battle-ready. How have uncontrolled circumstances in your life helped shape you? Can you see a correlation between your experiences and your attitude about things? Does your faith help you find a good balance?

2. Max is ready to come home. He needs to face the past and he wants to help his adoptive parents. The mix of emotions takes him by surprise. He's in uncharted territory and even being a covert operative doesn't prepare him for the raw feelings he experiences coming home. Did staying away so long help or hinder Max's healing? How can we tell when removing ourselves from a situation is helpful or self-defeating?

3. Tina is instantly attracted to Max and resentful of his past actions. He never came around after Pete's death. She finds that reprehensible. And then to stay away from his wonderful parents for over a decade? Unforgivable. But Tina learns that forgiveness is clutch in family and friends. Have you ever had to swallow your pride and ask...or give...forgiveness?

4. Jenny Campbell has taken on a new role, as caretaker for her sick husband. How tough is it to handle the ups and downs of caring for someone with a potentially life-threatening illness? Have you faced death with someone close to you? Did your faith in God help?

5. Tina's relationship with her aunt and cousin is challenged by the truth. The Gospels tell us "the truth will set you free," but sometimes that's easier said than done. Have you ever pushed yourself to be honest, only to have it come back to bite you? What would you do if you had the chance again? Would you make the same decision?

6. The joy of Christmas can weigh heavy on people going through a tough time. Loss, divorce, injury, illness, mental health issues...all of these can weigh heavy on people at holiday time. How can we help refocus the beauty of Christmas on the simplicity of a baby in the manger, a child born to the poor? Do you think making Christmas more sacred would help alleviate the pain it causes some people?

7. Max has the wonderful and difficult opportunity to be present during his father's last days on earth. This can be a time of healing and mixed emotion. When faced with similar circumstances, what can we do to help? How can we be "Christ" to those in need?

8. Max's Christmas gift to Tina was a leap of faith. He refinished her scorched tables and chairs, offering her the opportunity to stay not just through his word, but through his deed. Why was Max's thoughtful gift so much nicer than a fancy necklace or bracelet? And wouldn't you love a fun patio set just like that?

REQUEST YOUR FREE BOOKS!

2 FREE INSPIRATIONAL NOVELS
PLUS 2
FREE
MYSTERY GIFTS

Love Inspired®

YES! Please send me 2 FREE Love Inspired® novels and my 2 FREE mystery gifts (gifts are worth about $10). After receiving them, if I don't wish to receive any more books, I can return the shipping statement marked "cancel." If I don't cancel, I will receive 6 brand-new novels every month and be billed just $4.74 per book in the U.S. or $5.24 per book in Canada. That's a saving of at least 21% off the cover price. It's quite a bargain! Shipping and handling is just 50¢ per book in the U.S. and 75¢ per book in Canada.* I understand that accepting the 2 free books and gifts places me under no obligation to buy anything. I can always return a shipment and cancel at any time. Even if I never buy another book, the two free books and gifts are mine to keep forever.

105/305 IDN F47Y

Name	(PLEASE PRINT)	

Address		Apt. #

City	State/Prov.	Zip/Postal Code

Signature (if under 18, a parent or guardian must sign)

Mail to the **Harlequin**® Reader Service:
IN U.S.A.: P.O. Box 1867, Buffalo, NY 14240-1867
IN CANADA: P.O. Box 609, Fort Erie, Ontario L2A 5X3

**Are you a subscriber to Love Inspired books
and want to receive the larger-print edition?
Call 1-800-873-8635 or visit www.ReaderService.com.**

* Terms and prices subject to change without notice. Prices do not include applicable taxes. Sales tax applicable in N.Y. Canadian residents will be charged applicable taxes. Offer not valid in Quebec. This offer is limited to one order per household. Not valid for current subscribers to Love Inspired books. All orders subject to credit approval. Credit or debit balances in a customer's account(s) may be offset by any other outstanding balance owed by or to the customer. Please allow 4 to 6 weeks for delivery. Offer available while quantities last.

Your Privacy—The Harlequin® Reader Service is committed to protecting your privacy. Our Privacy Policy is available online at www.ReaderService.com or upon request from the Harlequin Reader Service.

We make a portion of our mailing list available to reputable third parties that offer products we believe may interest you. If you prefer that we not exchange your name with third parties, or if you wish to clarify or modify your communication preferences, please visit us at www.ReaderService.com/consumerschoice or write to us at Harlequin Reader Service Preference Service, P.O. Box 9062, Buffalo, NY 14269. Include your complete name and address.

LI13R

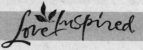
Keira wished she could keep her hands from trembling as she handled Tanner's saddle. What was wrong with her?

Seeing him again, his brown eyes edged with sooty lashes and framed by the slash of dark brows, the hard planes of his face emphasized by the stubble shadowing his jaw and cheeks, brought back painful memories Keira thought she had put aside.

He looked the same and yet different. Harder. Leaner. He wore his sandy brown hair longer; it brushed the collar of his shirt, giving him reckless look at odds with the Tanner she had once known.

And loved.

She sucked in a rapid breath as she turned over the saddle on the table. Tanner seemed to fill the cramped shop.

Keep your focus on your work, she reminded herself.

"So? What's the verdict?" Tanner asked.

"I don't know if it's worth fixing this," she said, quietly. "It'll be a lot of work."

Tanner sighed. "But can you fix it?"

"I'd need to take it apart to see. If that's the case, two weeks?".

"That's cutting it close," Tanner said. "Is it possible to get it done quicker?"

Keira would have preferred not to work on it at all. It would mean that Tanner would be around more often.

It had taken her years to relegate Tanner to the shadowy recesses of her mind. She didn't know if she could see him more often and maintain any semblance of the hard-won peace she now experienced. Tanner was too connected to memories she had spent hours in prayer trying to bury.

"I'm gonna need it for the National Finals in Vegas in a couple of weeks." Tanner continued.

"I heard you're still doing mechanic work, as well?" She was pleasantly surprised she could chitchat with Tanner, the man who had once held her heart.

"Yup, except last year I bought out the owner. Now I'm the boss, which means I can take off when I want. I took over the shop in Sheridan after a good rodeo run. The same one I started working on before—" He didn't need to finish. Keira knew exactly what "before" was.

Before that summer when she left Tanner and Saddlebank without allowing him the second chance he so desperately wanted. Before that summer when everything changed.

A heavy silence dropped between them as solid as a wall. Keira turned away, burying the memories deep, where they couldn't taunt her.

But Tanner's very presence teased them to the surface.

She looked up at him to tell him she couldn't work on the saddle, but as she did she felt a jolt of awareness as their eyes met. She tried to tear her gaze away, but it was as if the old bond that had once connected them still bound them to each other.

Will Keira agree to fix Tanner's saddle?
Pick up HER COWBOY HERO to find out.
Available January 2015, wherever
Love Inspired® books and ebooks are sold.

Love Inspired

JUST CAN'T GET ENOUGH OF INSPIRATIONAL ROMANCE?

Join our social communities
and talk to us online!
You will have access to the latest
news on upcoming titles and special
promotions, but most important,
you can talk to other fans about your
favorite Love Inspired® reads.

 www.Facebook.com/LoveInspiredBooks

www.Twitter.com/LoveInspiredBks

Harlequin.com/Community

LISOCIAL